I0771439

TAMARA HENSON

SOLANA

Pathos, Book 3

2nd Edition

Tamara Henson

Tamara Henson Studios, LLC

Barbourville, KY, USA

Thank you for supporting the creative work of
Tamara Henson!

Published by Tamara Henson Studios, LLC
Barbourville, KY, USA
www.tamarahenson.com

ISBN-13: 978-1-968677-04-6

DEDICATION

To Susan, who first pointed out that all the people in my head are just facets of my personality, my life, and my psyche.

As with any gem, some facets shine more vibrantly because of the surrounding darkness.

Love you!

*   *   *

CONTENT NOTICE:

This work mentions and depicts violent parental death, accusations of arson, ideation of arson, verbal and physical (non-sexual) abuse to a child by adults and other children, physical and emotional neglect, child elopement into the wilderness, and an unfavorable view of a particularly horrible fictional orphanage. Also, don't get attached to Smudge the Ragdoll...

CONTENTS

1: STORYTIME

A tiny house glowed warmly in the autumn golden hour. From the outside, it looked simple. Plain. Just a slightly run down house in the country on barely a half-acre of land. The eaves freshly mended, siding replaced and awaiting paint, the old house got patched up by a hardworking man who young Solana had grown to love as a father figure. And love, paired with her sweet mother, made that little house a home.

Solana's real father left four years ago, nearly half her short life of almost eight. When she tried hard, she could remember his face, his hazel eyes and his auburn hair and freckles. Mama kept one faded photograph in a frame for Solana, making Solana wonder if she remembered the man or merely memorized the picture. She'd stared at it for long hours, after all, studying his sun-squinted eyes, the serious tilt of his pressed lips, the wild arrangement of his longish red hair. Captured in a candid moment, like those old movie posters of James Dean, lacking only a cigarette and carefully styled hair.

Her mother glanced wistfully at the image every time she entered Solana's room, often making subtle comments about how Solana had his same color eyes and wild spiky hair, or how she held her mouth the same way when she was thinking hard. Her tone seemed so distant and sad. Solana caught her mother wiping away a tear once, and felt from her a sorrow she hadn't noticed before. Then Solana hid her father's picture in her sock drawer, face down under all the socks, so he couldn't make her mommy cry anymore.

His voice eluded her still. The timbre echoed in her head now and then, a distant echo or a ghostly laugh. Frustrated, though try as she might, she couldn't hear the words or focus enough to clear up the sound in her mind. *Being sad or angry for something outside your control doesn't befit blessed little girls*, her mother often said with a telling smile that didn't rise to her eyes. *Leave the sadness for grownups and just be happy.* So this little girl pushed down the sadness she felt, and let go the frustration, to be strong for her mother. A hollow, fuzzy sort of confusion remained.

Her mother said she'd explain it all when she grew up, so Solana would decide for herself if she needed to be sad at that time. But according to her mother, her father hadn't died. Just left. And Solana had not been to blame. Her mother confirmed that much. Hating the sadness in her mother's eyes, and confused and angry about why her father would leave such a good woman, Solana decided to be happy enough for both of them!

After a few years of sad sighs and staring into the distance, Solana's mother met the man she married last year. He had been in the military for years and shared a similar sadness in his eyes that matched her mother's in a way Solana couldn't put her finger on. Solana, though apprehensive at first, liked him well enough. The best part was, he made her mother smile, all the way to her eyes!

Solana spent some time pondering in her head how she should address the man. Would her mama like it if she called him Dad? Or should she keep calling him Archer? She'd given up on calling him by his weird first name Sephandrum; Alcourne, his surname, just made her giggle for some reason.

At long last, quite by accident the first time, and to Archer's delight, Solana called him Dad. She'd frozen as the word slipped out, incredibly self-conscious and embarrassed. He didn't seem to mind, if she could trust his beaming smile. He may have really liked it, though a sad murkiness seeped into that smile at first, clearing as time marched on.

Staring upward at the shower nozzle and sighing into the prickling water, Solana considered her many blessings and wondered at how such a good man made his way into their lives. As she would hit eight years old tomorrow, she announced an end to her traditional bathtime with her swimming mermaid float and rubber duckies and colorful bubble bath soap and artsy tub markers. She had reached the age of infinity, she told her mother, because her age turned on its side made the infinity symbol. At this age, she decided that great leaps into the future must happen. First, she gave up bathtime, her third favorite pastime, and replaced it with luxuriant showers. Then she told her mother to please stop cutting off the crust from her sandwiches, sure that important nutrition for growth rested in their dark, smooth surfaces. At this rate, she'd be shaving her legs in no time!

She kept drawing, her second favorite pastime, but aimed for improving that skill with fiendish focus. And her dolls still demanded the occasional tea party, so she couldn't deny them. But her favorite thing ever, stories, both reading and writing, she refused to give up! Imagination gave Solana entire worlds to explore, and people to meet. No amount of growing up could pull her from that joy!

Her mother laughed indulgently at her daughter's whims, assuring her that none of these changes need to happen so soon. Solana turned off the shower, sure that she rinsed off all her mother's sweet-smelling body wash. Then she stepped out onto the mat, looking for her towel.

The small house's tiny bathroom opened into the hallway, with both bedrooms directly perpendicular to the bathroom. Solana, dripping across the floor, peeked out to see her mother stoop with a grunt. She tidied Solana's small bed. Her belly swollen with Solana's baby brother, she struggled with things like that for now. Therefore, after careful consideration, Solana decided to grow up sooner. *Mama needs help now and after the baby comes.* And she needed to be the best big sister she could to the little boy. She needed to teach him how love works, how strong girls are and how much they matter in his life, so one day, when he has a family of his own, he'll know better than to leave.

Her mother gathered a half dozen thick storybooks into Solana's dingy yellow backpack and laid it on the floor beside the nightstand. Turning down the blanket, she laughed at the girl's ragged cloth doll. Solana had tacked her out with a paper knife and machine gun, a wide ammo belt with hand-drawn bullet slots each with a little red dot, and a headband made of red construction paper before settling her on the pillow for her nightly protection duty.

"Solana! Story time!" She turned to catch Solana dripping in the floor, staring at her. "Get in there off my hardwood floors! Shoo!"

"Story time, Dad!" Solana cried from the bathroom, echoing in the small house. Maybe Archer couldn't be her real father. That didn't matter. He treated Mommy like a queen and an equal. That's all she really cared about, all she required of anyone in her short life—to love her mommy like she did. But he treated Solana nice, too! "Mommy? Where's your big towel? It's fluffy!"

"Up top, Little!"

Solana tiptoed and pulled down a big towel from a high shelf, dragging several more with it. Then she paused to push the fallen towels back onto lower shelves. She draped the fluffy towel over her head and climbed to peek into the mirror. She practiced her smile. Her freckled cheeks dimpled; her hazel eyes sparkled. Eyes that matched her estranged father's. Her smile faded. Solana, though she didn't remember him much, wondered where her first, real daddy had gone. She wondered if he felt scared of her, like her pediatrician had been scared. She'd spoken in full sentences too young, possessed reasoning skills far beyond her age, understood feelings and picked up on emotions with shocking clarity. *Smart like your father*, Mommy said on occasion, with that same weird sadness in her voice. She wondered again why he left, then pushed it down and away, as she tried to obey her mother's wish for her to be happy.

Taking a deep breath, Solana pressed down her musings. She ran into her bedroom, her pudgy fingers clinging to the huge white towel that trailed behind her on the floor. Her mother snatched away the white towel with a laugh and pulled the ruffled gown over Solana's dripping hair. She smiled at the scrunched up face of her baby girl as she scrubbed her drenched hair with the towel.

"Hurry, Dad! The towel monster is getting me!"

Solana pulled a hat over her wet locks before her mother could attack the hair with a brush. Solana giggled all the while. Her mother finally sighed heavily and plopped on the bed, frustrated.

"I want to do it!" Solana cried and held out her hand for the brush.

Her step-father — a tall, broad-shouldered military man with short white hair and piercing blue eyes — walked in, wearing a worn green tank top and tactical pants. His long cord necklace with the small white spiral, which Solana loved, hung from his neck, almost to his navel. Barefoot, as always, he propped his shoulder against the doorframe and crossed his arms over his chest. Her mom stared at Archer's silly grin and sighed again, knowing she'd have no help from him.

Solana just wanted to prove she could do it, that her mother didn't have to. But it seemed her mother struggled with letting that little bit go. She always said Solana's thick, spiky hair made a rat's nest if not brushed.

"Do you have to go to bed wearing that old cap?" her mother asked, brandishing her brush threateningly. "At least let me finish brushing your hair first!"

Solana reached for the brush again. With a comical look of concern, her mother relinquished the brush to Solana. Solana laid the hat aside and started brushing her hair, cringing along with her mother as she pulled through each knot with force rather than her mother's gentle prodding. But her mother didn't interfere. Solana returned the brush to her mother once her mousy wet hair hung relatively straight and knot-free. Then she patted away the excess moisture like she'd seen her mommy do. Then as her mother took her towel to hang it in the bathroom, Solana crammed the blue ball cap over her wet hair.

"Solana!" her mother said with a sigh that quickly fell to a chuckle. "You are a treasure and a challenge to my nerves."

"But a treasure nonetheless," said Archer. His rich, deep voice made Solana smile. She felt safe and soothed. "Why do you wear that old thing to bed?"

Solana clamped on to it with both hands. "It's the first thing you ever gave to me."

"You heard her, Terra." Archer laughed again, adjusting the narrow black-rimmed glasses on his nose. "She likes my gift better."

"If that's the way it works," her mother said. Her hands moved at her throat for a moment, untying a deep purple ribbon there. "Well, then... It's time that you got a present from me. Your birthday is tomorrow, right?"

Solana went silent and sat next to her mother, nodding emphatically. "I'll be eight, finally!" She held up eight fingers for emphasis, a stern and serious expression on her face. Being able to count on both hands had been her privilege for almost three years. She would soon run out of fingers! "Practically grown."

Her mother took Solana's open hand and turned it palm up. "This is precious to me, so I know you'll take good care of it." She placed the silver heart in her hand, took the tiny key and showed her how to open it. Solana gasped at the tiny pictures inside. Her mother pointed to the picture on the left. "This is baby Solana! Look at those precious hazel eyes," her mother said, and pinched her cheek lovingly. "And this is Dad and Mommy."

Solana pointed to Mommy's swollen belly in the photo, "And this is my little brother Balor!"

"Yes, little lady," said Archer. "It is." He flipped the bill on her cap and sat down beside her. He closed the locket and tied the ribbon loosely around Solana's neck.

"Thank you, Mommy!" Solana beamed, sitting stiffly, not sure how to properly act while wearing real adult jewelry.

"You're welcome, dear child," Terra said, kissing Solana's forehead. "Let's settle down now for the night."

She scooted aside the ragdoll to make room. Solana lifted her for Archer's approval.

"Wow!" Archer took the doll. "Smudge is well prepared to protect you tonight! What are those red dots on the bullets?"

"Critical duty rounds," Solana said, proud that he noticed. "So they expand fully when they get to squishy areas, rather than getting twisted in heavy fabric. But I didn't know if they made them for machine guns."

"Good girl. Critical duty is for handguns, mostly. They make something like that for machine guns. I'll show you pictures tomorrow."

"Archer!" Terra cried out. When he met her gaze,

she stared open-mouthed.

"What?" Archer answered. "She picks up on things."

"Things that you tell her!"

"Might as well live aware." Archer shrugged. "All these weekends we've gone out into the mountains, she's learning and doing all kinds of stuff. She's pretty amazing at picking up skills. How to forage for food, make shelter, purify water, build a fire. Bushcraft stuff that everyone should know. And eventually, when you're comfortable with it, I'll teach her to shoot safely."

"You're right, of course." Terra smiled down at Solana. "She's the smartest kid I know, and you're teaching her some awesome skills. But we'll hold off on shooting for now. She's still my baby girl."

"I'm practically grown!" Solana spoke up. She brandished her eight fingers with an indignant expression, surprised by how quickly they'd forgotten.

Her mother laughed, and assured Solana that she had grown quite a bit. "But you'll always be my baby girl, even when I'm old and gray!"

Solana smiled past the mist that rose to her eyes. She couldn't imagine a day when her mother would seem old to her, really old. The foreign twinge in her gut screwed her stomach into a knot. Then Solana willed it to relax. She nodded and hugged her mama, tucking in Smudge the ragdoll close to her side.

"Now, it's story time!"

Her mother lifted a large, thin book from Solana's backpack and opened it to the front page. "The Unicorn and the Lake," she read. She flipped to the richly illustrated story pages and, taking a deep breath, began the legend of the unicorn and the serpent with barely a glance at the words on the page.

Long ago, they all memorized the text of Solana's favorite book, so often it had been repeated. And long ago, they had begun embellishing and extending the story in flights of fancy that captured Solana's attention and imagination more than any of her other stories. Story time in Solana's home became a warm affair full of the love of family, the bright, creative mind of a young girl, and the comforting embrace of familiar, epic adventures.

"Why doesn't the unicorn just fight the serpent in the beginning?" Solana asked again, putting up her fists to emphasize her personal resolve.

"Because she wants to give him a chance to change his ways," her mother answered. In this retelling, Solana reimagined the male unicorn as a girl. Her flowing mane and tail tangled with flowers and trailed new growth of greenery with each step. Solana explained that she could be pretty, creative and destructive.

"But she could save so many if she just kicked his butt when he first did the bad things!"

"I'm sure it hurt her that she couldn't save them all," her mother said, trying to make a different observation.

"Maybe," her dad answered, tweaking Solana's nose, "she wanted to believe in the good of the worst one, just like we believe that everyone can choose to do the right thing."

Solana mulled that over in her head, wishing desperately that the Unicorn could find a way to save them all, including the Serpent. Her mother continued the story, but this time the Unicorn fought hard to save everyone and tried to reason with the Serpent to avoid any more pain and sickness. In the end, Solana dozed with the book clutched close to her heart, so she didn't hear if the Unicorn's new approach worked. She sure hoped it did!

Her mother tucked the blanket in over the book, turned off the light and joined her husband at the door.

Archer hugged Terra tightly. Then he pulled the door together, whispering goodnight.

2: INFERNO

Solana smelled the smoke before she felt the heat. She sat up in bed, flattening her body against the headboard. Drowsy, unsure that she was even awake, she watched the fire devouring her small bedroom. All around her bed, the flames arose to engulf her. Detached, in shock, Solana saw flames creep along her comforter, flick across her toes, and leap onto the Unicorn book she held.

The back of the book caught fire quickly, searing away most of the cover and creeping inside to the last pages. Solana cried out and slapped out the flames with her bare hand. She gasped and looked at her palm. She felt the heat, but no pain. The remaining fire rushed in all around, burnt away her blankets and her clothes, and singed the bill of her old blue cap. She reached for Smudge, the old ragdoll on her pillow. The doll flared and blazed as the fire consumed her paper weapons first, then her thin, worn cloth skin.

Confused and terrified, Solana felt the fire press against her skin like a living thing. The flames tried to choke her when they couldn't burn her. She leapt to her feet on the bed and looked toward the window for a moment, considering the escape plan her mother practiced with her. But a gulf of fire separated her from escape. The great heat scared her but didn't burn her, couldn't burn her. She rushed toward the window, throwing caution to the wind with that realization. The living fire plucked her from the air as she jumped and pinned her against her headboard, hissing and roiling in impotent fury.

Her door crashed open and the shadow of Archer appeared, guarding his face against the blaze. The entire hallway appeared to be in flames as well. A soft white glow emanated from him as he forced his way toward her. The light pushed back the flames, but the flames shoved against him, too. Then another smoky figure appeared behind him—towering over her already huge stepfather—and dragged him kicking and screaming from the room like a small child. The fiery smoke monster—for that's how it registered in Solana's mind—seemed made of living fire more than flesh. Archer called out Solana's name over and over. Then cried out to Terra, her mommy. The fire answered with roaring anger and crackling laughter, drowning out his words.

Then the screaming started in the next room. Solana froze in her struggle against the flames. "Mommy! Dad! No!" She screamed over and over, wailing and crying over the roaring of the fire. But the screams of anguish and agony rose high above the sound of her own, until all too soon the noise stopped. Solana fell silent in terror. Indistinct shadows moved among the flames in the sudden silence, like shifting, formless smoke monsters.

Solana trembled in realization. Then she screamed and screamed. Her shrill cries continued to drown out the laughter coming from the fire. She sputtered and choked on the smoke filling the room. She grew dizzy and wobbled on her feet, but the fire continued to hold her back, mocking her and cursing her.

"I hate you," she spat out at the faceless fire, coughing uncontrollably. "I hate you!"

The fire lingered, almost quiet for a moment, watching her breathe in the smoke. Weak and helpless at last, Solana cried out, "Help me!"

A burst of color rushed from far away, increasing in her sight until it blocked out her vision. Roaring and whistling, the new fire of a million colors flung back the flame that pinned her against the wall. The new flame embraced her, whispering unintelligible comforts, and another word she didn't understand: *Taiyo*. Then, as wood crashed down in the hallway and a fireman spilled in around it, the colorful flame disappeared, leaving only the whimpering living flame behind.

Solana grabbed the strap of her sooty backpack in the second that the fireman stood astonished that she lived. Then he snatched her away and brought her quickly out to the waiting ambulance.

"Her health checks out," the paramedic said, shaking her head. "Her lungs are okay. She wasn't breathing in smoke for long. But you said her bed was on fire?"

"Yeah," the firefighter replied. He fretted nearby, breathing heavily from his exertions. "The floor, the walls, her blankets, mattress and frame. It was an inferno in there! Almost as bad as where we found *them*."

When Solana snapped her worried eyes to him, the man shut his mouth and mumbled an apology. "They're looking into the use of accelerants," he whispered. "But even then, the house wouldn't have burned so...so thoroughly in such a short time! I mean," and this he mumbled, "there's nothing but ash left of the man. The woman," he shivered. "I've never seen anything so gruesome," he said. "The fire spread to the surrounding houses in record time. So why are you asking about the bed?"

"Look," the medic said, twisting Solana's limp arm this way and that. "There's not a single burn on her entire body. Soot, yes. But no injuries at all! It's a miracle. You hear that, sweetie?" she said to Solana. "You're lucky to be alive!"

Solana felt the numbness creep over her body, choking her and nauseating her. Her too-sharp ears heard every word. Her body wouldn't move. Her mouth wouldn't open. She couldn't force them to understand about the smoke monster if she couldn't speak. Her voice wouldn't rise up and tell the woman that there's nothing lucky about losing everything ever!

"Take her to Sunny Creek until we can find her next of kin," he said, flipping through pages and pages of documents. "Looks like she should have a father alive, but he's estranged. We'll do what we can." He looked into her wide, intelligent eyes for a long moment before turning away.

The social workers showed up an hour later, giving Solana plenty of time to stare vacantly at the smoking shell of her small home. Firemen had extinguished the initial fire and worked to put out flames in the two adjacent homes. Some had returned to the site to put out the rekindled underbelly of the house. The crass man in the too-expensive suit whistled in surprise at the condition of the sticks that remained.

"No survivors from this house except this one?" He looked back and forth between Solana and the house. "No wonder. How are you doing, little one?"

Solana's stomach flipped at his singsong baby voice. Her haunted stare spoke volumes.

The man turned away, looking all around. "Wow! The whole neighborhood went up in flames! It's a wonder anyone survived!"

Solana felt the numbness waver a bit, but it held firm.

"Hush, Tommy!" A woman in a crisp white shirt slapped his arm. "Can't you see you're upsetting her?" The woman smiled at Solana, giving a sympathetic nod. "Ignore him. He's all dried up."

"Not seeing much upset, no." Tommy inspected

her again. She stared back as he turned her chin this way and that. "Maybe some shock, but that'll wear off."

"It isn't that easy, Tommy," the woman said. "I'm Shelby Ellington. I'll be your caseworker, sweetheart. We'll get along just fine, right?"

Solana paid no mind as Shelby Ellington wrapped the paramedic's blanket around her shoulders and hefted her onto her hip. Solana ignored the long car ride, but coughed on occasion. The only feeling left was the burning in her lungs.

3: LOSS

A disdainful smile greeted Solana. The spider-fingered, dark eyed woman who provided it had practiced a lot. It didn't reach her eyes, though. That smile almost made Solana feel scared or worried. Probably the first gift every child received at the Sunny Creek Working Home for Wayward Children. Such a cold, calculated smile proved to be the only thing freely given there.

The smile fooled the man who brought her here. He greeted the woman like an old friend, taking her hand in a courtly gesture and shaking it gently.

"Seems we have a quiet case tonight, Tommy." Solana stared up into the woman's mask of judgment and felt every last needle of her gaze cutting into her chest. "Are you worried, dear? Scared? No need. This Home will keep you safe. You'll build character and a good work ethic through structure and discipline."

"Ms. Battelio," began Shelby, who cradled Solana on her hip, "it's important for you to acknowledge that this is not a behavioral case, but an orphaned girl with no fault in entering that status."

"No fault, you say?" Battelio scoffed. "She seems plenty old enough to light a match."

"The evidence in the fire marshal's report will be conclusive against that theory, Ms. Battelio." The woman bit off the older lady's name with an acid tongue.

"She is not intended for the disciplinary program you employ for older kids. In fact, statute…"

"Calm down, Shelby." Tommy stepped up, his hands spread in a nervous gesture of peacemaking. "Ladies, please! This has been a challenging and truly upsetting night for many reasons, and emotions are high. I know Shelby doesn't mean to dictate your business to you, given the long term success of your program and your consistently high markings during inspection, Frances."

With those statements, Tommy fixed Shelby with a warning glare. Shelby opened her mouth to speak again, though better of her reply, and closed her mouth in resignation for the moment. She shifted Solana to her other hip, giving the little girl a full view of the woman named Frances Battelio.

The head coach—Sunny Creek's long-term coordinator and undisputed ruler of the Home—looked down on Solana's soot-smudged face. Artificial sympathy twisted her face, though her black eyes stared out, not an ounce of emotion rising there. Her fingernails, artfully filed into claws to accent her long, bony fingers, tapped a rhythm on her slender hips. She posed there, tall and arrogant, dressed in a blouse with a starched collar and a long pencil skirt, with hair severely slicked into an updo, hair to feet dipped in shades of gray. The scent of stale cigarettes and floral perfume assaulted Solana's nose. The woman stacked her angular body in a precariously teetering pose of highborn regality, appearing every moment that a stiff breeze would carry her away, much like the ash she resembled.

"That dreadful fire has made her an orphan of sorts, unless we find her deadbeat father," Battelio sighed. "Fire killed her parents." Solana cringed. "The same fire damaged every surrounding house in the already poor district. In places, the fire still rages, I'm told?"

"The fires are out, far as we heard," Tommy replied, nervously laughing. "There are only a couple houses adjacent to the property, and they only suffered minor damage."

"I'm sure that all involved will seek government compensation for their losses." Battelio breathed the words in an airy, condescending way. She paused to smooth her sleek hair against a sudden unmoving wind. "More leeching off the government on the way! That part of the county is known for it. I've raised many of their children while they abuse government services!" scoffed the woman with a frown that reached deep into her eyes.

Shelby spoke above the gloating tone of Battelio's words, not entirely controlling her anger as Tommy instructed, explaining the ordeal as she understood it, and providing a family history they pieced together. Battelio nodded wistfully, half-listening as the workers pushed past her into the foyer.

Battelio turned her attention to the blanket-wrapped child in the Ellington woman's arms. She left dark handprints wherever she touched the woman's crisp white shirt. Her dark eyes looked fearful in their smeared frame. Her light brown hair lay limp, drenched in sweat. In one small hand she gripped the strap of a ragged backpack that looked too heavy for a child to carry. The girl clenched it to her side in a death grip. The child looked out, unseeing. She couldn't have been more than eight years old. The Headmistress saw the potential for a hellion in the girl's white knuckled grip of the bag, and that unresponsive behavior. When Solana stared up at her, the woman's eyes were full of challenge, saying "I can break this one". Solana shivered again. Perhaps she was scared. Possibly, she was merely cold. Not much else felt warm to her, with the light drained out of her world.

"And above all, until we set up sessions with the psychiatrist, be sure to address her grief. Let her know

it's not her fault and she didn't do anything wro..."
Shelby said. She swayed with the girl in her arms in
some attempt at soothing her. Glancing past the
Headmistress, Shelby felt surprised by the silence of the
house, the chilling absence of activity in a house full of
kids, late night or not. The doorbell had rung. Surely it
would've awakened a few curious ones. "Ms. Battelio,
these are important instructions. Are you...?"

"Miss Ellington, is it? I assure you. I've handled
such cases since you were in diapers, so I know how to
deal with her. My goal as an educator is to create a
productive member of society, to love the children in my
care beyond anything else," Ms. Battelio said, her frown
fading as she reached for the child. "I've promised that
much to the state many times."

"And how often have you delivered on that
promise?" Shelby fired back, pulling Solana out of the
woman's reach.

Ms. Battelio pulled her hands back, acting
stunned at Shelby's words.

"Shelby!" Tommy said. "What are you implying?"
He swept his hand out toward the coach. "I know you
haven't lived here long, but you need to know. This
woman is a pillar of the community!"

Tommy leveled Shelby with a stern look, giving
her a nudge toward Ms. Battelio. Reluctantly, Shelby
allowed the woman to take the traumatized girl from
her. She watched, helpless as her gut churned with
apprehension, as the older woman stroked the haunted
face with her bejeweled, red-clawed hand.

"There, there, girl. Granny's here..." the woman
murmured.

"She's just new to this job," Tommy said as
apology. "She'll get the gist of things in no time. We'll be
off now, Frances. Be seein' you at the next inspection,"
said the superior.

"Congratulations on your pending promotion.
And I'll be waiting graciously as always, Tommy.

Regards to the missus," she said with a nod. "You both have a pleasant evening!"

She ushered them out and eyed Shelby with a pleasant smile. The door had barely closed before Ms. Battelio's hand stopped mid-caress.

"Now, girl, the first thing I'll do is get this filth off you."

She hauled Solana up a flight of stairs and plopped her on the commode in the hall bathroom. She began by taking off what remained of the girl's tattered, seared clothing while running some nice, steamy bathwater. When she tried to take the backpack from the girl, she met her first resistance. A firm slap to the girl's face loosened her grip on the strap. She whimpered once. The child never made another sound as the older woman threw her backpack into the corner. Ms. Battelio claimed her first victory.

She hefted Solana and plunked her down into the bathwater. Steam billowed from the surface of the water. Ms. Battelio had let the water get far too hot for a simple bath. Solana clenched her jaw, feeling like she would boil if left in that water for long. Still, she didn't react outwardly. *My skin hurts, but I just don't care.* Solana slowed her rate of breathing, carefully controlling her pain, pushing it down. She felt terrified that the woman would hit her again. *At least I'm feeling something.* She didn't move, even when her skin turned bright pink and looked ready to pop. What had the woman wanted? For her to scream and pass out? *Or just to see me show pain? That's ridiculous. What a cruel trick!* Solana instinctively knew Battelio had done this very thing before, and determined not to give her the satisfaction of knowing how much the hot water hurt. Score one for Solana's willful unresponsiveness.

Battelio took a rough cloth and scrubbed at Solana's dirty face to reveal pale skin under the soot, except the heat and friction left it pink. Thankfully, the scalding water cooled to a tolerable heat by this time.

The water became murky as Battelio finally soaped up Solana's hair. Even the old woman gasped in surprise. She'd thought Solana's hair mouse brown. Each of her three scrubbings revealed orange hair that grew successively brighter, with blond and red tints throughout.

Solana felt Battelio's discomfort rise, with a feeling akin to fear. Solana already realized the reason. *The only survivor from a house destroyed by flames possessed hair the color of fire.* She hadn't been the first person surprised by Solana's natural hair color. She was the first to react with fear and coldness. Score two for Solana's resolve to do whatever it took to survive in this twisted place run by a real, tangible monster.

4: RAGTAG

Four years passed since her imprisonment at the Home when her parents died in the fire. Four years of fighting subtly against Battelio's many abuses.

At first, Solana felt nothing. That first strike to her face registered, but not much. The scalding water hurt her body, but her mind shut it off. She couldn't even remember if her skin blistered, since the heat from a fire didn't even consume her. But until that day, no one had struck her in violent anger and bitter, unfounded hatred. And on any day before that, she may have reacted with tears. But she hadn't shed a tear since that day. The fire may not have been able to kill her, but her insides felt like an empty husk toward almost everyone she encountered.

When Shelby took her to the first psychiatric appointment, she still hadn't regained her voice. Several appointments later, the nice old lady behind the desk coaxed from her the first words she'd spoken in weeks. "They died. The smoke monster took Dad. And it's my fault. That is all."

The lady probably thought she spun some elaborate hyperbole or simile to describe what happened to Dad. But no, she had meant it literally. She didn't doubt what she saw. She just felt sure of her guilt in the process.

Through the months that followed, the psychiatrist helped Solana realize that she had not started the fire in her home. The investigation returned no fault by the inhabitants of the house; neither Solana nor her parents could be found at fault. Solana realized instantly what the woman didn't say—that someone else had indeed been in her home. The smoke monster, person or creature, had indeed been present and not just a figment of her imagination. And the first real feeling she regained echoed her last feelings toward the fire. She hated it, as much as her innocent spirit could hate. However, that feeling, she kept to herself. The desire to seek out the smoke monster and see the life drain from its eyes, she kept to herself. And soon, within just a year of weekly counseling, the psychiatrist released her back exclusively to the Home and her struggle with absolute solitude among children who outcast her. And to Battelio, who hated her for something she did not do.

Solana continued to bear the brunt of Battelio's fury for the first three years, taking each strike, kick and verbal aggression in stride. She learned to force down any reaction so the bitter old woman would neither have cause to rejoice nor to provide additional cruelty as punishment for talking back.

Several times, Battelio piled the clean dishes from all the cabinets back in Solana's dishwater because she "wasn't washing them fast enough" for her liking. She scrubbed walls as punishment, only for Battelio to snatch the chair from under her feet for "missing spots", causing her to tumble across the floor, bruised with a broken bone in her hand. When asked sarcastic rhetorical questions, Solana got accused of mumbling curses under her breath, which warranted more retaliation. Forget for the moment that Battelio lost so much of her hearing in recent years, it's a wonder she heard anything. Every spoken word, she accused of a mumble. When every word could be twisted into a lie to those deafening ears, Solana chose silence.

Solana learned to stare ahead silently and trudge along the path of metaphorical broken glass and eggshells Battelio laid before her. Every bruise, cut, or broken bone had a formulated excuse behind it that she must relay to the case workers if asked. And Solana knew she must never reveal her emotional scars to anyone. The social workers must see her as simply an adventurous if clumsy little girl.

One day, after years of bearing the full brunt of Battelio's abuse, Solana snapped. She felt the constant haze of apathy, fear, and oppression clear in an instant. She didn't know the final trigger. It could've been something small. The woman had her polishing the brass rails in the upper hallway that overlooked the sitting area where would-be families came to visit the Home's potential adoptees. No one sat down there at that time. Otherwise, Solana wouldn't be seen by the public doing such hard labor in the Home. Feeling the old woman creep up behind her, Solana glanced warily out of the corner of her eye and continued working.

Battelio slid a white gloved finger along a portion of the rail Solana hadn't polished yet. The glove picked up the slightest tarnish. The old woman shoved her gloved hand under Solana's nose, where only a minor smudge discolored the glove. She buried the fingers of her other hand in Solana's thick hair and yanked her to her feet, cursing every second about Solana's nonexistent laziness.

"You're a liar!" The words sprang from Solana's mouth. Her anger surprised her, so long had she kept it suppressed.

"What did you say to me, you little brat?"

Solana's belly erupted with heat. She ignored the pain of the woman pulling her hair. She twisted to face the woman and threw down her rag. "You lie to the social workers, you lie to the inspector, you lie to the state, and you lie to us kids!"

"You are all worthless!" Battelio yanked on Solana's hair with such force that she stumbled forward.

"My mother always says...said that no one is worthless. That each life matters." Solana clamped her hand over the old woman's wrist.

"Your mother is dead! And you killed her!" Battelio screamed, trying to wrench her hand free of Solana's death grip.

Solana's vision went black at that moment. She roiled in emotion that robbed her of reason and crushed her carefully cultivated control. *Your mother is dead.* Solana's heart thudded. *And you killed her!*

"No," Solana said, in a voice so quiet that she doubted the woman could even hear her.

Then vivid colors of vibrant light flooded her eyes, with the word Taiyo flowing through every ember. Heat and flames exploded from Solana's body, seeking to burn her adversary, Battelio. Solana clung to the sound of the old woman's screams, trying to stay awake. Then Solana crumpled to the ground, unconscious.

Solana awoke in the Cell, in complete darkness, as usual when she misbehaved. Her ribs felt sore and her arm and wrist ached with bruises. Battelio must have kicked Solana over and over once the fire on her face went out. The old woman's hair never grew back in that one spot. She hid the burn scar with makeup on the side of her face. But luckily for Solana, Battelio's rule about handling everything in-house applied to herself as well. Battelio never mentioned that fire nor Solana's house fire, nor how either started, perhaps sure that no one would believe her. But after that incident, Battelio never beat her again. She only used her words and conditions to hurt Solana, but wisely kept her mother out of the conversation.

Outside on a bright day, Solana closed her eyes and breathed in the brisk air that heralded the end of summer. The coolness whirled through her lungs and out across her lips. Not too long from now, the vapor would hang frozen in midair when she breathed. Her stomach gave a flutter of excitement. Finding peace outside in the cooling air, with the fading sun high overhead, Solana settled on the sidewalk beyond the crumbling walls of the prison behind her. Sunlight flashed off Solana's pale skin and flame-colored hair.

On her lap lay a huge book entitled *Legends of the Unicorn and Other Fanciful Creatures*, inches thick and one of the few things that survived the fire that destroyed her home, and the smoke monster who killed her parents and baby brother. Two more books lay by her side: *The Lore of the Unicorn*, an encyclopedia of sorts, and her burnt children's book titled *The Unicorn and the Lake*. She still loved the latter. The ending had been charred where she clung to it on her burning bed, rendering the last pages unreadable. The children's book had been the one story she memorized completely. However, try as she might, she couldn't remember the words. The psychiatrist told her that her memory and the ending would return to her in time, as the trauma settled in her mind. She glanced briefly at the book, feeling the heat of fire that didn't burn her, smelling the searing of flesh from beyond the hallway. Trembling, she tore her eyes away and back to her open book. Without looking that way again, she shoved *The Unicorn and the Lake* down into the patched and ragged yellow backpack that held all her salvaged books.

Solana forced her mind back into the story, away from the fire and the smoke monsters and the death of all she held dear. She tilted her chin toward her chest, her fiery hair curling and spiking wildly from pigtails to frame her intent face and wide hazel green eyes. She turned pages quickly, reading fast and pausing appreciatively at the beautiful illustrations. This time reading the book, she could almost see the flowing white hair and blue eyes of the creature as it pranced through the forest, laying its great head on a fair maiden's lap, and the fierce horn and sharp hooves slashing as it battled the serpent and its other enemies into infinity.

"Kid, Miss Ellington is here to speak with you," said Sara, the kind-faced cooking coach. "She's waiting in the office. Come on."

Solana closed the book and tucked it into her bag before heading to the office. Miss Shelby Ellington sat all prim and proper, in a crisp white blouse and a long, close skirt. She wound her long brown hair into a tight bun, aging her beyond the twenty-something she must be. From her earlobes dangled pearls on strings of silver. Solana noticed over the years that the social worker had the habit of tugging on her earlobe when she felt stressed.

When Solana walked in, Shelby released her earlobe and hugged Solana close to her. She murmured how much Solana had grown and how good her grades were, even though it had only been a couple weeks since Shelby's last visit. The one-sided nervous banter continued until Solana grew uncomfortable.

"You asked to see me," Solana said, her voice cautious and soft.

Shelby shut her mouth, nodded, and said, "I have news for you."

Knowing Ms. Battelio would be nearby, Solana whispered, "About my father?"

Shelby nodded again, gesturing that Solana should take a seat beside her. *That means the news isn't good*, Solana thought. She'd been asked to sit down for news too often in the last four years. Her aunt said she already had too many kids and couldn't take her. Her mother's parents—her grandparents—continued enjoying a long retirement in their cabin and didn't have the resources or energy to raise another child. Her stepfather's parents were long dead, and her father's parents had not returned any messages. She had felt alone and lost for years as every family member joyfully signed over their custodial rights. Only her estranged father remained, about whom she knew nothing except an old photograph and the gleam in her mother's eyes. And even that memory faded.

"You got married to that nice Gerry guy?" Solana eyed the new wedding band on Shelby's ring finger, her eyes crinkling with real happiness for the nice woman.

"Why yes, I did!" Shelby answered, her fingers reaching for her earlobe before she snatched her hand back. She dropped her hand and reached instead to twist and turn the plain gold ring on her left hand. "He's a peach. The best ever, except..."

"Except what?" Solana asked. Solana felt her stomach churn. Her gut said something is wrong. Why wouldn't Shelby tell her?

"Well, nothing really. That's enough about me, so stop changing the subject. This is important for you!"

Solana gulped past the nervous knot in her throat and took a deep, calming breath. She stared, waiting, into Shelby's brown eyes, past the perky façade, and to the truth. Shelby felt so sad about something, and she didn't want to talk about it. Her eyes looked puffy and red under the simple, carefully applied makeup. Solana wondered what could make her cry so much, if she felt so obviously happy to be married.

"Stop that," Shelby said, unnerved. "That knowing look you have, it's really something!" Then she smiled to cover her emotions. "We tracked your biological father to a small community in England, so he's overseas. He's backpacking on some long-term sabbatical, according to his passport records. So he'll be hard to find until he resurfaces, yet it seems he always comes back to this one small town in the north, and visits a family by the name of Alcourne there. Authorities in the region are in possession of documents they can serve when his name pops up again. Then he can contact us!"

"Only if he chooses to, right? What happens if you can't find him?" Solana asked. Her heart pounded in her ears. "If he doesn't want me either?"

"Then the state will dissolve his parental rights, and you'll continue to be a ward of the state," Shelby said, the apology thick in her voice.

"A ward of the state," Solana whispered, her heart burning within her. "Not so long ago, I was a daughter to good parents. That's all I really want again, is to be someone's daughter." Solana's eyes pleaded with the woman, though she pushed down the hope and words she wanted to express.

Shelby said, "You know if I could, I would take you as my own in a heartbeat. It's just more complicated than that. This whole system is harsh and unforgiving, especially to the older children."

Solana dropped her gaze. She shoved the hope down deep inside again, feeling foolish that it arose at all. "I understand. Almost twelve is pretty old, anyway, I guess." Her heart sank to her feet, knocking the wind out of her.

"That's not what I mean," Shelby said, trying to salvage her slip of the tongue. "If I could adopt any child, it would be you. But...but the truth is, Gerry wants us to have children of our own, to carry on his name. And after the...the complications we had this last time we tried, he's not sure we should even have children."

"Ah," Solana said, realization rising above her pain. "That's what it is. The sadness in there," Solana pointed at Shelby's eyes, "is because you lost a baby."

Shelby stared wide-eyed at Solana for a long time, considering a lie. But Solana had never been wrong when reading her. "That's true," Shelby admitted. "It hurts very badly."

"I know," Solana said. Her voice cracked with emotion. "See?" She opened her silver locket for Shelby. She pointed to her pregnant mother's belly. "I lost one, too. I was gonna teach him every story I know, and everything I ever learned," Solana said, her expression wistful. "But when I think about it, I don't really know much at all that really matters. So he wouldn't have learned much."

"No," Shelby said. "He would've had a wonderful big sister, Solana."

She hadn't been a good one, though. Not yet. Good sisters act on things and move things forward. Something clicked in Solana's head and began to work back and forth in her mind, forcing out her desperation with plans of action. She didn't have the right to ask anything more of Shelby. The woman had enough on her plate. Solana realized that hers must be only one case among many. But Solana had spent too long doing nothing and allowing others to change her life. She didn't know what something she would do, but it would have to be big. Her world hadn't been changing in the right ways, so she'd have to change it herself. She covered her mixed emotions with a smile.

"You'll be a great mommy someday," Solana said, pushing down her feelings in a show of strength, "just like you've been a great worker for me. Thank you for that."

She ignored the embrace Shelby offered, hoping the woman didn't notice how final those words sounded. She jumped to her feet, grabbed her bag, and swept out the door, skipping her goodbye hug this time. A great swell of a dozen emotions ripped her heart apart. She couldn't stop the tears when they started. She tried to muffle the sound as she ran down the hallway. She made it to the bathroom before Battelio heard her crying.

Safely in the small hall bathroom, she locked the door behind her. Solana curled up by the tub—where Battelio scrubbed her raw and tried to burn her with hot water on her first night—and cried her eyes out, cramming her mouth against her sleeve for silence. Deciding to change things, she realized, is almost as hard as the longsuffering silence and self-control she had employed since arriving at the Home.

When her crying-shudders subsided, Solana ran cold water for her face and swollen eyes. Nothing could hide the fact that she had cried. The red rims and puffy eyelids made the green in her hazel eyes glaring and bright. She would have to stay scarce or risk some type of retaliation by the workers, or Battelio, or even the other kids. Especially the other kids. She needed to avoid any further punishment-inducing incidents. When she felt sure Shelby had left, she snuck past the coaches and to the playground. She hid in the shadows, in an alcove near the building, so she could calm her very busy mind with her books.

Solana, once bubbling and vibrant, now behaved as Battelio expected—though the old woman proved increasingly fearful of the little girl. Solana pushed down everything—her desire to kill the smoke monsters who took her parents, her horrible treatment by the narcissistic, abusive Headmistress, Shelby's rejection— and forced an appearance and behavior devoid of outward emotion. Her mother always said Solana seemed wise beyond her years, reading and writing early, understanding things she shouldn't without being told. She planned on using that insight.

Beyond her in the high-fenced playground ran ragtag children, all unwanted like her and dealing with it in their own ways. Solana, flipping pages in her book without reading them, knew she, like them, seemed a hairsbreadth from despair. She rubbed her burning eyes with the back of a hand. Her former life may have been hard, her family poor, but they gave all they could and loved her exceptionally well. Her current life held such drama that she only wished to rise above it, with or without Shelby. The fleeting expression of a deep-seated desire to have a family, the idea that Shelby might take her home, had been a pipe dream anyway.

The children all around her missed families they barely remembered. Some had parents who still lived, but had lost their children due to drug use or other illegal activity. They dreamed of going back to a home that didn't exist for them, at least not safely. Others held onto dreams of finding their place in the harsh world. And still others expected great things from the world to fall into their laps. Solana despised these kids most of all, as they felt entitled to something without working for it. Solana decided she would actually do something to make things happen on her own, now that everything else fell away. And her father? Well, she no longer had time to wait on a dream that may never happen.

The only thing her father had provided to her, her name, came even before she arrived. She wondered how he knew her then. But Solana's mother once said her father had a way about him, whatever that meant. She told Solana she knew the name seemed perfect from the moment she first held her newborn baby girl and looked into her auburn-streaked green eyes framed by wisps of yellow, orange and red. Baby Solana smiled the most genuine and beautiful smile her mother had ever seen. The smile reminded her of rays of sunshine sent to warm her heart. Solana, the name of sunshine, stuck.

Thinking about her name brightened Solana's eyes. Shelby said that her biological father visited a family by the name of Alcourne in England. Archer's surname, Alcourne. She wondered if Archer knew her father, but that seemed absurd, as she felt sure he would've mentioned it. Then she realized it wouldn't be something he might tell to a little girl.

Regardless, Archer's long lost family may have ties to England, meaning she had ties to England by her mother's marriage. The ties wouldn't be blood, but maybe they could tell her something about her father, and if she should try to talk to him. She never heard of another person named Alcourne. By her logic, trying to talk to that distant family might at least be a way to better understand her deceased stepfather. Her thoughts and plans consumed her as she sought out a way to meet those possibly distant relatives.

Solana glanced up at the children in the barren playground. They climbed on the old wedding-cake style monkey bars and stomped around a tall wooden platform perched atop metal ladders. They slid down a fireman's pole in the center of the platform. Some played ball in the open, flat part of the field. Older kids huddled at the top of the hill, lounging on a wide, flat rock and sneaking cigarettes when the Coaches turned their heads.

The residents themselves presented a microcosm of challenges unique to Solana's situation. From the older kids, Solana learned where she could get drugs and alcohol, how to smoke and spit and many other things little girls shouldn't know. They berated her for flatly refusing their wares, even though she kept their secrets better than most. The younger children lived in a separate wing, enjoying what Solana hoped were conditions far above her own. She stayed away from them all when she could, as her reputation regarding fire spread fear among the kids. Solana's heart, over time, filled with a permanent loneliness, except for the fading brightness of Shelby's visits.

She read, talked little except in answer to the Coaches and Battelio, and preferred to be invisible to the other children. Her plan worked well, except on bright autumn Saturdays when her namesake cast conspicuous light on her variegated hair and freckled skin.

"Whatcha readin', girl?" Rex began innocently enough, flashing a chipped front tooth with his thin-lipped smile. "Nice book ya got there, Red. Mind if I...?" he trailed off as he reached for the book. Without losing her place, she turned sharply to the side, slipping the book out of his grasp. *I thought I was better at hiding than this!*

"Amazing how someone so small thinks her stuff's better'n ours. We could take it from her, and prove our point," said Gin, a skin-and-bones girl with flat, thin blond hair, whose alcoholic mother abandoned her a scant three years ago.

"You two should be able to read before you bother stealing books," Solana growled, shutting the book with a pop. "Or you can both do me a favor and go away. Spare yourselves the embarrassment of looking even stupider than you already do."

"Are you calling me stupid?" Rex loomed above her, clenching his fists.

"I'm just saying," Solana sighed, "if the stupid shoe fits, you'd wear it. No question."

Solana spun up to her feet and, grasping the book, placed it in her bag. She flung the weight of her bag over her shoulder and settled it on her back by tugging the straps. She needed no more incidents now that she had this plan developing in her head. However, when incidents gravitated toward her, she knew better than to back down.

"You should think about how you talk to us, little girl!" Gin reached out and snatched her arm. "You're the stupid one if you think you're not going to pay for talking back!"

Rex grunted in agreement and grabbed her arm on the other side, with a much tighter grip than Gin's bone-thin fingers. Short for her age, Solana stared up at them as they towered over her. She had no trouble pulling her arm down and free from Gin's feeble grasp. Gin fell sprawling forward onto the sidewalk, crying out in frustration and pain. Others noticed the commotion and came to watch.

Rex clung tight, squeezing her wrist until it hurt. She couldn't yank her hand free even though she tried. Solana refused to scream in pain though. Rex wanted that, to hurt her. He had talked all the time about how to hurt things, to the point where even Solana shut him up with her fist in his mouth. She reached for his eyes with her free hand, willing to dig them out with her chewed-on nails. Rex leaned his head back out of reach.

His eyes glazed over and a smile spread across his face.

"Oh, look!" Rex said, noticing her red-rimmed, puffy eyes. "She's been crying again! Time to give her a real reason to cry." He squeezed again and she heard a muffled pop, a fresh dislocation in her own wrist.

Her eyes disguising her anger, and teeth clenched in pain, she glared at him with detached disgust. She dug the fingers of her loose hand into the back of his fist. Then his free hand wrapped around her throat. Still, no one offered help, not even the older kids. Solana panicked, kicking and scratching weakly from lack of air. Black splotches blotted out parts of Rex's glee-filled face. Blood rose to her eyes, filling her vision with its crimson radiance. Then a flicker came from within her mind, seeming far away, like the glimmer from a flame. It danced before her and soothed her. *Am I dying?* she asked the glimmer. She felt herself floating there, not knowing whether she was airborne or if Rex had lifted her by her throat. A dim voice came to her mind then.

"Your death lies much farther ahead than you can imagine, child," a lilting voice whispered in her mind. "Your soaring heart will guide you along an unraveling thread of many paths. Seek this thread and time will bring you to your fate."

Solana's ears crawled with fluttering vibrations, sending unnerved shivers down her spine. The odd vibrations gained and joined into a cacophony of shrill piercing cries and rumbling roars. Solana felt the familiar tingling in her limbs descending through her fingers. Brilliance burst all through Solana's sight in flames of purple, blue, green and red. The fire of Taiyo descended through Solana, driving shadows from the darkness around her. The flames surrounded her and caressed her pain-wracked body into blissful unconsciousness. Her body fell limp upon the yellowing grass of the schoolyard.

5: TAIYO

Solana awoke from weird dreams of soothing peace, wholly unlike the night terrors she usually experienced, with a word on her lips.

"Taiyo?" she rasped. *Where is she?* Her throat hurt and her wrist ached. When she tried to flex her wrist, sharp pains shot up her arm. She laid upon a rough blanket in a close, pitch dark room with a rectangular beam of light glaring in from what she knew to be a door.

"Yes, that's the word you said before. A curse in another language, perhaps?" spoke the nasal voice of Ms. Frances Battelio. "The injuries you caused the children have landed you in the Cell again. We've got to make up our costs in treating them somehow, and I can effectively deprive you in here."

Ignoring the woman's biting words, Solana rubbed her eyes. "What happened?" Solana asked, swallowing hard past the dryness in her throat. Her voice felt like razors slicing from the inside out.

Silence answered her for several minutes. Battelio must be contemplating her own experience with fire in Solana's presence. "You don't expect me to believe that you remember nothing, again? It's a nightmare. And the reports to their social workers? What a farce! You're aware that I prefer to handle all issues internally." She paused, waiting for Solana to speak. Battelio took heart from the girl's silence. "However, I'm afraid if we have one more incident from you, your pyromania will go on your written record."

"No, please," Solana whispered in a rush, gulping past the pain in her throat. Solana knew she didn't start fires, at least not intentionally. "I don't remember. Rex hurt my wrist and choked me. That's the last I remember."

Battelio laughed derisively. "Consider how that sounds to an adoptive family, coming from a child whose par..." The woman wisely stopped, clipping the words off rather than provoking Solana by mentioning her parents. Her fingers flew to her scarred face. Solana scowled up at her, seething, wishing she could call down fire on purpose. "Consider the concerns an adoptive family would express," she continued, more wisely but just as cruelly.

"I consider everything, Coach," Solana snarled. "Constantly." She opened her mouth to continue, but bit her lips closed to regain control of her emotions. Solana hated the musty darkness more than physical retaliation. However, a written pyromania report would ensure that no one would ever take her into their family. Her heart pulsed in time with the throbbing of her sore throat. Then she remembered her age, and how Shelby told her that most children in her range age out of the system before adoption. In a further panic, she patted the floor around her. Finally, her uninjured hand closed on the worn strap of her yellow backpack.

Casting her fearful, cruel, cold gaze through the small rectangle of light, blocking half the light with carefully coiffed hair that hid her burn scars, Battelio missed nothing of the action. As Solana pulled the bag close for comfort, Battelio mocked, "Yes, you have your precious books. We would have taken them, but you hugged them so tightly and pathetically we would have had to break your other wrist to get them from you. No large matter. Books are useless without the light to read them." She chuckled to herself as she closed the creaking shutter. She paused, venom dripping from her forked tongue. "And the next time you decide to burn something, try destroying yourself and save us this trouble and expense."

As the shutter closed at last, Solana thought better than to say that the fire wouldn't hurt her, couldn't burn her. Solana heard children through the metal lined door. They yelled "Freak!" and "Monster!" and the various obscenities their hard lives had taught them. Solana cried then, in confusion and wordless agonies, hugging her beloved backpack full of books to her chest and drawing up her knees to cradle her bag and head. Sobs wracked her small body, sending vocal shudders out of her mouth into the muffling fabric of the backpack.

Hours passed. Solana's heart settled. She'd cried into exhaustion. She felt more swelling in her cheeks and eyes from their drenching. She eased onto her side, still curled protectively around her damp satchel. Utterly exhausted, she didn't even want to read anymore. Lacking light, she couldn't read anyway. Sleep would not come. Never in that darkness had sleep come easily. Time distorted there. Senses distorted. Solana heard the occasional rattle of the ancient ventilation system as it pumped fetid air through the hand-sized vent far above her head. All else stayed silent and dark. *Plenty of time for thinking.* Then her wrist sent a twinge down her arm.

Solana sat up, wiping strands of moist hair from her eyes. From her backpack she pulled a small handheld flashlight she'd sewn into the lining. She called it Anti-Cell. She clicked on the light and dug out a couple chewed pencils. Then she ripped from her knee length pants two bands of cloth. She laid those across her lap and began feeling around the swollen joint, picturing the bones and ligaments in her mind from anatomy books. Solana grabbed the backpack strap and shoved it between her teeth.

She felt the two parts that were not in place, then grasped around her wrist, twisting until she felt the bone and ligament settle into place beneath the swelling. She bit off a growl of pain. A wave of nausea swept over her. But the overwhelming pressure eased. Quickly, she tied the pencils as a splint around the wrist, drawing in her breath with each new pain.

She began to remember the lady's voice from her dream. Under her breath, she whispered the word *Taiyo*, feeling the strange word roll from her tongue and wondering at its meaning. The peaceful dream felt so real, and odd to one so accustomed to uncomforted night terrors and fragmented memories.

The Taiyo lady mentioned her destiny. The dreamer in Solana wanted to believe in destiny, in a fate taken from her reaching hands and placed under the authority of a competent higher power. But her faith had always been action-based. She never felt entitled to anything but a loving family. She always kept her mind active. Do the thing yourself! Rise to meet the challenge headlong. Bash yourself against the wall until you break through! She set her mind to tasks and achieved them, and attributed their many results as either learning experience or success. Or perhaps her stubbornness and headstrong nature made her less accommodating to the idea of fate.

No matter at present. She couldn't deny that Taiyo existed. She remembered the soothing timbre of her voice, like the whispering of a cheery campfire. Taiyo had never spoken full sentences before. Solana hadn't heard more than her name in the past incidents, and that was more of a feeling than a spoken word. Taiyo's instructions came across as more of a confirmation of her need to run away. The voice had said, *It begins now.*

SOLANA

Solana decided to heed her active subconscious, or this external entity. Now she knew which big scary thing she had to do. Finally, she planned the details of her escape into the uncertain, terrifying, wonderful future.

6: FAÇADE

Battelio granted Solana leave from the Cell a day later, on her twelfth birthday, conveniently right before inspection that day and visitation the next. Solana played the perfect submissive tenant. She allowed one of the women to scrub her down and dress her in clean, worn clothes. The water felt tepid by comparison to her first bath in the same room. Solana still cringed whenever she saw a bathtub. Only nowadays, Battelio steered clear. But the other coaches insisted on helping her, on making sure it was done right. *At twelve, I am perfectly capable of bathing myself.* Her wrist didn't throb as much, and seemed to stay in place well. She held her hand under the hot water to soothe the hurt away. She could flex it with little pain.

"Stand up straight. Dry off your hand. My, it looks bad. Try to keep it covered." Solana nodded. She would do what she was told for now.

Another woman brushed her bright hair and pulled it behind her head in a tight ponytail.

"It just spikes out too much when you put it in pigtails," the older woman said. "We must have you looking all neat and clean in case someone comes to adopt you tomorrow."

Solana blinked at the woman's well-meaning words. *You mean I can't look unruly in case it gets you in trouble*. Solana held her tongue. Tact would be her ally if no other would. She decided to hide her books and pack inside a secret cubby hole she knew from her years of roaming the halls of her prison. She determined to also take some of the non-perishable food whenever she got the chance and hide it in the same place.

"Wouldn't that be *nice*, child?" the woman said in a loud voice. She had apparently been talking to Solana while she planned. Solana muttered "yeah" under her breath and got a cold smile that told her she'd given the right answer.

The Inspector arrived shortly thereafter. It was now Tommy, freshly promoted. He had a different assistant this time, someone Solana had never seen. Shelby had been reassigned, he admitted in a conversational tone. When he asked her about her swollen wrist, she lowered her head and didn't respond. She pretended bashfulness as she'd been told.

Ms. Battelio waved it off with, "Oh, you know how clumsy children can be. She's probably embarrassed that she tripped on the playground."

He grinned and nodded at her in that condescending way adults had. She stared back blankly. He would be no help to her. Even his new assistant greeted Solana warmly. But she was no Shelby. Deep in her mind, Solana fought a rising panic. *Why was Shelby reassigned?*

Later, when the Inspector and his assistant left, Solana thought she caught a glimpse of Shelby heading toward Battelio's office. Solana couldn't be sure it had been her because she seemed oddly distant. She didn't smile the same way she once did. And she wasn't wearing her crisp white blouse. When she tried to get close enough to eavesdrop, one of the lady coaches steered her away toward a waiting chore.

As Solana cleaned part of the kitchen that night, the cooks whispered something about a miscarriage for that lady. *"She was worried she may have to adopt."*

Solana cringed. Her heart sank at the word *worried*. The women all agreed she probably wouldn't want a broken child. Solana bit her tongue, her mind raging against them. Solana realized how cruel these women were in all their ways. But Shelby had been here! In her heart, Solana knew Shelby was a sweet woman. She would be a good mother someday.

Solana let herself drift for a moment with the possibilities adoption would bring her. She considered a warm home and a new family, a new mother named Shelby. Then she remembered her conversation with Shelby just a couple days prior. She remembered her mother and stepfather. They couldn't be replaced. Even her estranged father was out there somewhere. Maybe he would come back for her someday after all. Her stomach flipped. *No*, she thought. *I have to do this on my own!* She decided it was best that Shelby wouldn't be attending the Home anymore. She had proven far too perceptive and knew Solana well. Solana had things to do that would be suspect to Shelby. She tried to bury her dreams of a new family and focus on the destiny Taiyo presented.

The next day proved challenging for Solana's newfound focus. Couples came the next day to scout possible children. Ms. Battelio wrapped a scarf around Solana's bright hair and sent her to a distant bedroom for cleaning duty. If the Head Coach wanted to keep her away, the work did not seem difficult enough.

Soon she finished and returned to the railing overlooking the meeting area—a huge room with a wraparound balcony on the second floor. From upstairs, she looked down on the large room with its cushioned couches and secluded corners. A few couples had taken aside orphans to "try them out" by talking with them. Solana smiled at the bright faces of the children who'd known desperation. Some of the rougher, older kids had given up hope and left the room. Her heart sank as she sensed real heartache in their gruff actions. She reached up and untied the scarf that covered her hair and made pigtails with the bands she kept around her wrist. She watched the activity below with keen eyes.

A familiar face caught her eye. In the far corner of the room, sitting on a green couch, was a woman with dark hair, a woman Solana almost dismissed because she was out of uniform. Shelby Ellington's smile seemed sweet as always, her eyes still sad and haunted. A tall man with blond hair sat beside her. He held a toddler on one knee—a red haired menace who kept reaching for the man's glasses. The boy had been birthed by a teen mother who'd spent most of her life in the Home; she came back pregnant after running away a couple years ago, then gave birth to the child and ran away again. The women called him Seth.

Solana stared with her mouth open and her hands tightening a pigtail. The realization took hold and sorrow leapt into her heart. *If I could adopt any child, it would be you*, Shelby had said just a couple days ago. Then why were they visiting Seth? *What did I do wrong?* They'd wanted a baby all along, not an older girl. Tears leapt into her eyes. Four years of rejection and abandonment had not prepared her for the shattering in her heart she felt.

Shelby glanced suddenly up at her, as if she felt Solana's gaze. The woman's eyes widened when she saw the sweet little girl to whom she had been so kind. Solana blinked back the tears and cast a wide smile at the woman. Shelby didn't smile back. Her eyes were a strange combination of alarmed and sorrowful. She hadn't expected to see Solana at all. Solana blinked again and nodded at the woman.

She turned tand fled back to the room she'd cleaned. She cried again, so happy that the sweet woman might rescue that little boy before he could be scarred by this place and so sad that they hadn't even considered her in the end, after all Shelby told her. She regained her composure the moment she realized she had been followed.

Ms. Frances Battelio walked through the open door and ran a gloved finger around the edge of a dresser. Her finger came back clean. Disappointed, the older woman knelt and did the same to a corner of the floor. Her finger remained white and clean. She grumbled to herself as she pulled off the glove and shoved it in the pocket of her long dress. She approached Solana, who sat on a corner of the bare bed with her hands in her lap.

"I saw you watching the Ellington woman," she began in her sweetest voice, easily a trap. "She seemed very happy with that little boy."

Solana nodded.

"Did you think she would prefer you, perhaps?"

"No, ma'am," whispered Solana.

"Good, because she did ask that I bring you out for her."

Solana's heart stopped at the old woman's light tone. She shot Battelio a cautious, wide-eyed look. Hope and suspicion warred inside her. *Please, no!*

"Unfortunately, when someone asks to see a child, we are required to discuss at length any... problems that child may have."

Solana gulped. Her chest tightened.

"I just had to explain that despite appearances, Solana is just not a child I would recommend, because she had been a pyromaniac since she arrived. I then took it upon myself to explain each *incident*," purred the old woman. "Including this one."

She gestured to her face. The makeup gone, Battelio's burn scar glowed pink on her pale skin. The woman exposed her scar for spite! Anger arose in Solana's chest for the first time since her recent imprisonment in the Cell. Her face burned with a fury of surprising ferocity. *How dare this woman?* Solana bit her lips together, remembering what family had been like, and wondering if she'd know that feeling again. *She turned Shelby against me, even as a friend!*

"You might imagine that she was doubly shocked when I reiterated the theory that you'd caused the fire that killed your parents years ago," Battelio said. Then she made a disapproving clucking noise. "A pity, really. Quite a shame."

Solana raged internally, hiding behind her carefully cultivated façade, but she did gasp at this accusation. The old woman knew how to hurt her after all, without directly mentioning her mother. Wordless evils that should befall the old woman flashed across her vision too fast for her to comprehend. For once, she wished she could call down Taiyo's flame on her own. This monster didn't deserve her many comforts, the power she wielded against the innocent, nor her safety.

She forced a deep breath to calm her anger. She bit her tongue to keep any ill words at bay. A few silent moments passed while Solana roiled in painful emotion. Then she pushed everything down with a valiant, desperate effort. *Battelio can't know how this affects me.*

"Is everything all right, child?" asked the old woman, every word dripping with venom.

"Yes," she said, mustering all the strength in her small body to control her tone. Then truthfully, she said, "I am happy that the little boy will be given a chance at a new family. He is truly blessed." Solana smiled for his newfound home, despite Battelio's taunting.

Then Solana stood and, taking her cleaning bucket, continued toward the kitchen. She brushed past the silent old woman and continued on her way, ever diligent in her preparation to meet her destiny. She kept walking even when she heard Shelby call to her from the top of the stairs. Solana couldn't deny her involvement in any of the *incidents* Battelio outlined for the social worker. Solana couldn't pretend like flame didn't fascinate her, even though she'd never set a single fire on her own, except at camp with Archer.

Regardless of how Battelio spun it, Solana came out looking like a bad apple. She rounded the corner and headed full speed to the kitchen, ignoring the echo of Shelby's voice calling her name down the corridor.

Battelio must have caught Shelby, because she didn't follow Solana. Solana half-hoped that the social worker would come for her. But perhaps she stopped on her own, realizing that Solana wasn't the girl for her after all. Solana's stomach churned. She turned her mind away from the sore subject, and pushed the pain down deep inside.

She knew other homes for children may not be so bad. She decided that if she could survive such a place, however, that she could easily meet any fate. She made it to the kitchen and struggled with the bolt on the heavy old door. She saw an easy method of disabling the handle lock when the time came. She would figure out how to reroute the alarm system later. She poured dirty water from her bucket down the spout that led to the base of the hill.

She picked up the broom and began sweeping heavy dirt from the neglected sidewalk before it turned into mud. Something moved in her periphery and she snapped her head in that direction. Rex stood there watching her. His hair and eyebrows looked terribly singed from the event of which she had no memory. His eyes afraid, he approached her and tensely threatened her as usual, ready to run at any moment.

"Monster! You'll pay!"

When she didn't respond, he regained his vigor and hurled several rocks at her. One of the rocks busted her lip and chipped an incisor slightly. Several more left painful bruising and cuts. She maintained her hollow gaze straight into his soul as the blood dripped from her lips. Maybe the corners of her mouth turned up in a smirk. Maybe he saw the fire deep in her eyes. *I feel so much fear from him*. His lips trembled. His knees shook.

Solana merely wiped her mouth on the back of her arm and continued sweeping, content to remain a monster in his eyes. He left her alone after that.

7: SMILE

Weeks passed after that day. Thinking they'd finally broken her, the coaches of the Home entrusted more menial tasks to Solana, jobs much worse than any required of the others. She felt dirty and tired most of the time, but physically stronger in so many ways. She used the isolation and distance to train her body and revise her plan of escape. Battelio gave her a wide berth in those days, knowing how her calculated actions had damaged Solana and, Solana guessed, not quite sure how Solana would react over time. Solana didn't know either. Her policy of no-more-incidents had been easy of late, since the kids ran from her and Battelio left her to her sorrow. Leaving the place consumed her with absolute focus. Every move, every breath, each push of the broom led her toward freedom someday, and the destiny Taiyo promised.

News came to her in snippets from the adults. Shelby and her husband adopted Seth. Shelby found out she was pregnant a week ago, only to miscarry again. Tommy, the new Inspector, confirmed with Battelio that Shelby had been reassigned to allow more time for motherhood. Feelings ebbed and flowed in Solana's heart. Shelby suffered, and her mind reached out with a hollow, longing kind of ache. But since she couldn't even see or visit Shelby, she pushed that feeling down. She stayed the course. Solana kept her mouth shut and plodded ahead.

All the roiling emotion settled into silence in her chest. On a day when the coaches planned time at home with their families for Thanksgiving, Solana disabled the alarm system. Late that night, she recovered her duffle bag full of food and her backpack from the hole in the wall. She hung the heavy duffle bag from the bottom of her backpack and tied a strap around the back of it.

Then she grabbed her scant belongings and shoved them alongside her precious books in the tattered satchel, which she slipped onto her back with great effort. Testing the weight against her strength, she stooped and dug through the duffle bag to leave some things behind. But she needed all the food she could carry! At the end of November, going into December, she'd find next to nothing to forage. All Archer's careful teaching in bushcraft and foraging leaned toward advance stockpiling during the preceding months. Solana had only been able to do that with nonperishables from the Home.

She reasoned one food against another for a while, balancing one can against another bottle. She pushed aside a handsaw, a belt knife, a small shovel, a box of matches and some twine, but felt like she needed it all. At last, her hands shaking from the prospect, she realized what could lighten her load. With a heavy heart and trembling bottom lip, she offloaded her books one by one, staring at them one last time before pushing them to the very back of her hiding spot in the old building. *One day, I'll come back for them!*

Her small hands encircled the silver heart locket and key—once her mother's—and tied the ribbon choker-style around her neck. She patted it out of habit, then smiled a sad smile. Her mother had loved her broad, carefree grin, with her deep dimples and smiling eyes.

Solana paused to look around her, hesitant and out of practice with real goodbyes. So she settled for a prayer. She spoke into the darkness, the sweetness of her lilting words flowing in a high and low cadence like the speech of songbirds. Not everyone heard that tone of voice from the fire-haired little girl. Only when she spoke with complete love and devotion did the singsong words flow from her lips. Only to her parents and God, for now.

"I promise, Momma, to smile again, for you and Dad," she whispered. "'Cuz you gave me enough love to share," here she furrowed her smooth brow, "and I haven't been sharin' much since Yah took you home. I'll find someone who needs that love, and show 'em," she sighed into the quiet room and closed her eyes. "Yahweh, please let 'em know. Thanks. Amen."

She hefted her load again, with much less effort thanks to the lightened burden, and headed back to flip the final breaker that would turn off security cameras, signaling an alarm within fifteen minutes of power failure.

Solana pulled Archer's dirty blue baseball cap over her bright hair and slipped along the wall in the empty kitchen. With a hand-drawn map in her hand of the wooded countryside and the surrounding towns, she exited the building through the kitchen door, easily twisting the broken lock. She shut the door quietly behind her. Then she entered into the darkness of a snowless, bitter November night with her hooded jacket pulled tight around her, and hands jammed into thin pockets of hole-pocked jeans. The tenacious girl set out on her own. Her thin-soled sneakers crunched on the dry yellow grass as she left the open field and entered the wooded hillside toward freedom, and her promised destiny.

8: SOLITUDE

Solana ran as hard as she could for two days straight, stopping only when she crumpled in a heap with a stitch in her side. Then she would get up and run again. Another couple days of hiking found her more comfortably away from those who might come looking for her. Her new strength served her well on the long trek. She kept moving even when she felt tired, pushing her body to unexpected extremes. She believed that no one could, or would, travel far enough to find her after that. She felt so exhausted that she settled for her location just the same. Her journey left her deep in the woods, halfway up a mountain. Far away from the Home.

Solana scouted the area and found a thin stream that led to a fairly deep, clear spring in a small clearing. She reached into the clear water with her grimy hands and drank her fill. She knew she could survive as long as she had water. She sat down on a rock beside the pool and dug into her belt pouch for the remaining bread and cheese she had stowed. Dumping those last crumbs into her mouth, she sighed. Nothing remained for her to eat save the canned goods, some shelf-stable milk cartons, and a few apples she snatched from the kitchen. Luckily, she had stuffed the duffle bag with all she could carry.

Solana, blue cap still pulled tightly over her bright hair, found a small outcropping that blocked most of the cold winds. She spread her stolen sleeping bag right against the rock and piled all her blankets on top. Tomorrow, she would settle in. Tonight, however, she just planned to shiver to sleep. The howling of the wind woke her just a few hours later. She felt stiff and more tired than when she laid down. But she stood and stretched, forsaking the cocoon of warmth she had made with her blankets to relieve herself in the underbrush. *Not that anyone's looking*, she thought with a measure of defiant immodesty.

The pale eye of the sun coldly lit the frozen landscape before her. The temperature climbed for hours until the golden light edged all the dormant foliage with its radiance. Solana stood, bundled in her blankets, and soaked up the natural warmth of the sun. She knew little of the science behind weather, but in this region between November and December, she knew that such warmth was always followed with a cold front that could kill those who were out in it. So she needed some protection before the weather took a bad turn.

"Time to settle in before I freeze to death," Solana said to no one in particular.

She rummaged until she found enough saplings and branches to build her shelter. The hand saw proved effective hacking at the thin wood, even though it took a long time to fell the little trees. She used the small belt knife to notch and trim the wood. She stopped and sharpened the blade twice before she could finish. She dragged the longer saplings and set them to rest against the outcropping while she cleared the area of debris.

Near the stone outcropping, the ground felt fairly solid and mostly stone. Two standing trees dug their roots into the rocky terrain about five feet apart and a few feet from the outcropping. Solana eyeballed the top of the ledge, about four feet high, and used twine to attach a long sapling trunk cross-wise, a few inches below four feet up on each standing tree. Over this top edge, she tied more sturdy branches and thin trunks side by side, also layering the sides with branches to make a wedge-shaped skeleton. When she finished enclosing the structure, only a third of the front remained open, facing the shallow cup of the outcropping.

Solana gathered and bound layered pine branches on top for insulation. She tied down a worn brown tarp to shed water and the coming snow. The finished product wasn't nearly as pretty as the lean-to Archer had made with her on a camping trip, but it served its purpose. She paused, breathing in the scent of freshly crushed pine needles. The smell reminded her of Archer. In that moment, she missed him and her mother so much. She felt so thankful that he took her camping with him and taught her how to do survival things. Insisted on it, in fact.

A few feet from her new home, under the lip of the bare stone of the outcropping, she used a branch to scrape the forest floor bare to the dirt and stone. She pulled some heavy stones into a crude circle to make a hearth for her fire. Since the wind flowed over the outcropping, then over her house and down the slanted back, she decided a fire would be protected there. *Worst case, I'll burn down my rough home.* She gathered as much loose, dry wood as she could find and piled it next to her small lean-to house. Archer always said you need way more wood to make it through the night than you think, so she didn't want to skimp on the effort.

Solana, with smudges on her face and scrapes on her palms, stood back from her accomplishments with her hands on her hips. Her empty stomach immediately protested her hard work with a fierce growl. She put off eating for quite some time as she gathered fresh pine branches, inspected them for bugs—distrusting her knowledge that winter drove bugs into hiding—and piled them in the lean-to. She spread a thin blanket over her new bed and unzipped the sleeping bag over top.

Solana filled her water bottle from the cold spring and opened a can of soup to heat. She reached for the matches she'd placed in her bag and groaned. Water dripped from the bag. One of the water bottles ruptured and drenched all the matches she smuggled. Her heart sank. She poured out the matches near the hearth, setting them in a row on a rock. She only wasted a couple before she decided to try again when they had dried. Surely not all were ruined.

Ever productive, Solana plucked some dry, fluffy moss called old man's beard from the side of a tree and tucked it under a pile of tiny twigs from her kindling pile. Then she dug a small, empty cigarette lighter from her bag. Battelio threw it away because it ran out of fluid, but Solana grabbed it anyway. The flint striker still sparked. It took forever to get the tinder to catch with just the tiny sparks alone. Eventually, she had a happy little fire over which she carefully heated a can of spaghetti and meatballs.

She stared down at the food halfway through eating. *How much food will it take to get me through spring, when I can forage better?* At that moment, Solana realized two things. She would have to control her eating or risk starvation, until she could grow or catch her own food. And she had no intention of returning to civilization. Definitely not the Home. Oh no! Not that place.

Maybe she would still seek out her father overseas, though she couldn't see her way to that option yet. But she knew Archer taught her how to survive for a reason, and survive she would. This whole embracing fate thing is exhausting! Solana rubbed her eyes with the back of her hand and yawned, looking around at the half dozen tasks she needed to complete before nightfall.

She spent the rest of the evening weaving a door from twigs and weeds—complete with twine hinges and a working latch made out of a loop of twine and a bound stick. If her training held true in her memory, there should still be edible nuts and a few plants she could forage this time of year. She could make pine needle tea for some Vitamin C, though the flavor made her cringe. She could build snares for small game, knowing squirrels and rabbits still ventured out regularly. She cringed at the thought of ending a life to preserve hers. *Life works like this sometimes, though,* Archer said in her memory. He never ate much meat, but to survive, he would.

Her spoon scraped the bottom of her warm can of spaghetti. *This canned stuff won't last if it's all I eat.* She needed to gather as much as she could against the coming snow, or die. The sobering thought led her to glance upward, paying attention to the cold setting sun and the colors it sent blazing across the sky.

Darkness approached fast. She stoked her small fire and climbed into her lean-to, settling down onto her warm, soft bed. The stone rock facing reflected the heat directly into her tiny home, holding its own heat for a long time. Late into the night, her small fire died. She snuggled down deeper into the bouncy softness of the pine boughs, thankful every moment for Archer's extensive training. She awoke shivering and stiff all over, but well rested.

Solana pursed her lips at the cold ashes of her fire. She stretched and yawned, rubbing the sleep from her eyes. *I'll have to wake up a couple times at night to add wood to the fire, or I'll freeze!* Solana dug a deep basin to store her sports bottles full of fresh water. She packed hard clay from near the spring in the crevices of her lean-to to keep out the coldest air and bound more boughs to the top. By habit, she gathered and dragged wood back to her woodpile with each trip. Soon, her little camp felt homey and well-stocked in that way.

Solana stood with her hands on her hips, admiring her hard work. She knew the firewood wouldn't last the night, so she'd continue to drag out whatever fallen wood she found.

She settled into a routine that day, which kept her calm and sane. She worked at camp on a project, then went out to explore and forage, then returned dragging whatever she found with firewood under her arm or trailing behind, bouncing along the underbrush and dry leaves. With each trip, she busied her mind by telling a different story in her head or whispered aloud. She even told herself the Unicorn and the Lake story, though the ending still eluded her.

Feeling accomplished, Solana used a couple ceramic bowls to heat water to scrub her face and clean her scratched hands. The crisp air on her wet face took her breath. She frowned around her, feeling completely alone and considering finishing her cleaning outside. Finally, she took the bowl inside her small home to scrub the rest of her body, so she wouldn't feel naked in public, and so the wind wouldn't bite as hard. The dry, brisk air and a towel helped her dry quickly.

She sat by the fire on a flat log, warming her body. Archer always said sitting directly on the ground could be dangerous, because the earth sucks the heat out of you and lulls you to sleep, where you can easily freeze to death when the fire dies. He also said that sitting close to the fire all the time mesmerizes and lulls you too, so that you fall asleep and die when the fire dies. That kind of preventable death—by sheer ignorance— worried her and drove her to constant movement. She got up after just a few minutes of thawing out, moving toward the next task and the next, coming back often to stoke and feed the fire or add to the woodpile. That night, she jerked awake every time the temperature dropped, so she could feed the fire.

The next day, Solana ventured out on a long forage, risking the death of her fire to find food. Years in the orphanage had been difficult, terrifying at times, confusing, and hurtful. However, the only time she recalled complete silence was in the Cell. A dull anxiety had been gnawing at her the whole time, in silence, out in the open. Constant industry dulled the feeling. Just today, in the quiet of this trip, it scared her. The memory of silence in complete darkness chilled her to the bone. She shivered under the pale, wintry sun shining overhead. Her feet dragged in the fallen leaves until the stony shock of her flight set in, freezing her feet to the ground in fear. Solana had never endured so long in utter quiet. Her vision narrowed, and for a long moment she expected to fall unconscious.

A chittering, scraping noise above snapped her back to the present. Her eyes followed the noise. A squirrel scolded her six feet above her head, clinging to the tree facedown. His tail twitched this way and that, showing her how angry and intimidating he could be.

Solana slowed her breathing to an acceptable rate, placing her hands on her knees. Still, the little squirrel fussed at her. "So, Joe," Solana began, naming him decisively, breathlessly. "This nut-gathering business must be hard for you."

She wandered another mile from her lean-to before she found any nut-bearing trees. Solana kept walking then, creeping even farther from the tiny house she built, from her camp, and from her inviting fire. After Joe's tree, she told a whole story to herself before she headed back. She filled her backpack that day and planned a new trip for tomorrow.

Solana had to go farther to gather food the next day. But she stopped under Joe's tree on her way back through. "Maybe, you already got them all and I get the leftovers. Well, Joe, I better get home. It's getting dark."

Joe just *squack, squacked* at her, defending his hoard of nuts.

"It's not like I can climb up and steal them, you know," she scolded. "But if I could... it changes things when I'm surviving the same as you are!"

Solana faced her path and headed out. Then a nagging feeling caught her in the pit of her stomach. She turned back and, with a heavy sigh, dropped the backpack from her shoulder. She unzipped the top and dipped her hand into the pile of nuts she collected. At the base of Joe's tree, she dumped two little mounds of nuts. Then, begrudgingly, a third handful.

"There," Solana whispered. "I hope that helps, because that's all I can manage right now." Joe barked at her again, but she imagined that it was a bark of appreciation.

Her bag felt much lighter on her trip back the third day. Joe didn't bark at her that day, and she missed his noisy chatter. He was nowhere to be seen. She checked the tree base for nuts and felt pleased that he had collected every last one. She secretly hoped that didn't make him one of those layabout good-for-nothings Archer had talked about. Solana looked up at the white sky with its dark shadows and knew that he had to be curled safely in his tree, on a pile of nuts, sleeping away the coming Winter.

"I wish I could hibernate, too, Joe," Solana sighed. "Things would be much easier that way."

Solana shivered every step of her walk back to the tiny clearing. Twilight had fallen—the latest she'd ever arrived back at camp. She stalked around in the darkness, making sure no animals had entered her lean-to or invaded her space. She stood over her firepit, which now only slightly glowed with dying embers, sighing heavily. In her memory, her mother sang the phrase, *Sighs consume the heart's blood, dear!* It always came from somewhere across the tiny house, in another room. Solana always felt amazed that her mama even heard her sigh that far away. But clearly, she was pouting and whining. So she knew she needed to stop all the sighing and just get to work.

During this farther distance she wandered, the

fire had burned to ashes. She rushed to stoke the flames back to life and held her hands almost in the fire to thaw them out. Some dash of memory gurgled from her mind into her stomach, filling her with an insane desire to touch the flame.

She stared at her fingers silhouetted against the soothing light. Then she leaned forward, closer and closer until the whitest flames touched her fingertips. The heat flared through her hand. Reflexively, she snatched her hand away and pressed them against her lips. The heat faded as quickly as it happened. Then, processing what happened, Solana realized there was no burn, no injury. Only heat. Her brow furrowed in confusion for a second only. Then her pensive curiosity took hold.

Holding her hand flat above the flames, Solana passed her hand horizontally through the tallest flame, very quickly so she didn't get burnt. At that rate, even the heat didn't register in her palm. She dared slower passes deeper into the fire with no injury. Only the heat registered, and even that wasn't horribly jarring to handle. She fought the logic and training of her mind for long moments while thrusting her hand into the center of the fire and holding it there indefinitely. This she did until her sleeve caught a flame that flickered until she patted it out.

She sat there feeding wood to the fire for a long time, staring at the fire and dipping her hands in and out of the flames. She remembered, slowly and surely and disturbingly the last time she'd been surrounded by flames. Her heart gave a shudder as the fiery smoke monster took shape in her memories and walked out of her room, taking her parents from her.

Her heart fluttered again, bringing with it the kind of deep horror and rage that only real suffering can create. Her eyes refocused on the fire, with both hands thrust inside, clenched as fists. Sparks of multicolored flame leapt from the fire, casting blue, pink and purple over the small camp. Eventually, Solana's breathing returned to a low and slow hiss. *Taiyo*, Solana pushed hard with the thought of that name, *I'm here. I'm still here, and I haven't forgotten my goals.*

She stood and threw more wood on the fire. Solana stared at her hands and arms, which were only well warmed, not burnt. *Fire took them.* She knelt and crawled inside the lean-to. *But I know now that fire isn't the enemy.*

The image of the fire and smoke monster at the forefront of her memory, she busied her body and poured the third, smaller take of nuts into her stockpile in a corner of her little house. She rationed them as one of her two meals per day. She had collected a couple rocks to crack open the hard shells.

The dry cattails by her spring made great kindling for her morning fire, if the embers died before she awoke. And she could boil certain barks with pine needles to make a nasty tasting but nutritious tea. *No scurvy for this girl*, she thought, gritting her teeth. She blessed Archer twice for his teaching.

Thinking of her parents again brought a pain to her stomach. Her anger gave way to mourning. She wondered about them all that night, crying and praying and worrying and praying because she worried. She remembered her promise and only had Yah tell them the happy parts about her newfound freedom. She fought against sulking as much as she battled worry. And she didn't sigh once.

Solana kept her spirits up by daydreaming of the future. Someday, she would kill the smoke monster. She would ask it why it took her family and home away. Then she would make it pay. Anything beyond her day to day survival, and anything beyond killing the smoke monster, she couldn't really focus on. She believed in a higher power, but she believed she had to work hard to reach her goals.

When all the animals finally went away or slept

for winter, she was alone with no one to talk to except herself, aloud. She talked to her mom and dad and God daily, for her sanity as much as her soul. She looked for the silver lining to the thick white and gray clouds that gathered overhead, heralding winter.

Ignoring the occasional rumble in her tummy, the minor and major discomforts that winter camping brought her, Solana knew things could always be worse. She knew the blessings lie ahead, but also in each day. This whole survival thing wasn't that bad after all.

9: GOOD INTENTIONS

Days later, Solana returned to her little camp after a particularly disappointing trip to gather nuts. She scouted her perimeter and paused to inspect her lean-to. Something wasn't right with the door. She froze, afraid of the sudden rustling that came from her home. Reaching for her belt knife, forcing her breathing down to a rattle, she crept forward around the back of the lean-to. When she made it to the side of the door, she peered in and drew back with a squeal.

The animal inside gave a yip of surprise, then hissed. It rushed out and bore down on Solana as she ran away. Realizing she had nowhere to go, Solana ran around a large tree and turned, swinging the knife wildly at the oncoming animal, screaming as she did. She saw the thick, heavy paw swing at her leg, the claws long and flashing in the setting sun.

But then he wailed in pain, his many sharp teeth revealed in two long rows. Solana felt the resistance of her knife slicing into the animal's shoulder. His amber eyes burned into Solana's. The animal, a huge bobcat, turned and ran into the forest, his heavy paws thudding across the dry foliage.

She stood there gasping for breath. She kept her

hands clamped tightly on the grip of her knife. But then Solana fell, quaking in fear. Her adrenaline dissipated. Then her left leg started aching, so she looked down. The bile rose in her throat. So much blood! Her thin pants, shredded so easily, hung in tatters from the knee. And beyond her knee were four gashes, the top two deep.

Solana pulled off her belt and tightened it above her knee, stemming the flow of blood. She sat against the tree to calm her quaking insides. Her mind raced. She didn't have the proper medicine to treat such a bad wound. She had no more pants, or bandages, or anything of real use. She hobbled back to her lean-to, keeping an ever-vigilant hand on the knife and looking over her shoulder for the creature to return.

She warmed some water and cleaned the wound with a tattered shirt. The long scratches weren't as bad as she thought—no arteries severed—so she loosened the tourniquet, testing the blood flow. The wounds needed a better cleaning than she could give them, and some stitches in places, but the blood and plasma began clotting well after she cleaned it. She rinsed out the shirt in the bloody water, then wrung it out and laid it to dry. She removed her belt tourniquet completely, and waited again for the blood to flow. Satisfied that her leg bled only a little, Solana wiped the bobcat's blood from her knife. She wrapped another shirt around her leg and tied it snugly with strips of the same fabric. Then she crawled into her home.

In the lean-to, the bobcat had made a mess of her pine branch bed, tore her thin blankets, trampled her supplies dugout, and ruptured two of her soup bottles. The smell of urine was strong. Solana guessed she had interrupted him lapping up the soup, and he got scared. Her heart welled in her for the poor thing. *He was just hungry, like me!*

Seeing the ruined space, Solana sighed. Considering the circumstances, she thought a little sigh would be okay, even if it did consume her heart's blood! Between the wound and the mess and the pee smell, she sighed twice, maybe three times. *It's a shame we gotta be enemies now, Bob!*

She looked around, for the first time disgusted in her adventure's inadequate supplies. *I tried, but not hard enough!* She needed more food, more clothes, more matches and other supplies, and to have a doctor look at her leg. *It can't be helped*, she thought. *I have to go into town!*

With the problem of just how she'd get all she needed without money—and without getting recaptured—in the forefront of her mind, Solana tidied up her lean-to again, scraping the urine-wet dirt with a ragged branch and kicking the stinking dirt out her door in disgust. She then emptied her backpack and duffle bag into the supplies dugout. She'd need every bit of room to carry all she needed!

Darkness descended. She huddled near the fire, staring at her tattered hand-drawn map of the countryside and plotting her course for the morning. She updated the map with a cartoon cat and labeled it Bob. There was a town nearby, as far from Sunny Creek as she could find without crossing a river. She had already made it past two weeks on her own, so they'd probably think she was long gone by now. Or dead. Solana sniffled. Either way was fine by her. She settled down in her lean-to for a troubled sleep, full of slashing claws and gnashing teeth and stinky urine.

Bleary eyed, Solana awoke before dawn. She rubbed her swollen leg and thought better of treating it, since her shirt-bandage held fast. She grabbed her bags and map, then headed toward town.

Four hours of trudging took her to a long blacktop road through the woods. She had begun to wonder if she'd made an error in drawing her map around the time she realized she forgot to bring any food. Her stomach protested in anger. She shushed it out loud, startled in the silence. Relieved to see some signs of civilization, finally, she walked another two hours down that road. She hid from the one car that passed, but otherwise walked in silence and solitude. But her mind was a whirlwind of speculation.

The first buildings came into view, part of a small informal community on the outskirts of town. She took a moment to cram her bright hair under her blue cap and pulled the thin hood over her head. Solana's stomach churned with nervousness. The cold had long since numbed her fingers and toes, but caused her injured leg to throb. She struggled not to limp, as she knew that would draw attention.

She tucked her chin down, shoved her hands in her pockets and headed straight down the sidewalk. No one was out in this weather. The temperature dropped the longer she walked. She passed house after house undetected. The end of the sidewalk gave way to the town, and beyond that, a free clinic for the homeless— she hoped. She picked up the pace.

A large inflatable ball bounced across her path. Solana stopped in her tracks. She stared at the ball, then looked toward the source. She stared openmouthed at a small, cozy looking yellow home with a spacious front lawn covered in toys, at the small boy with red hair who toddled across the yard, and at the thin woman in a crisp white shirt who grabbed his arm and scolded him for trying to cross the street. Then the woman followed the path of the ball. She cried out when she recognized the little girl.

"Solana?" Shelby Ellington cried. She hefted Seth into her arms. "Oh my goodness! They've been looking all over for you!"

They, Solana heard. Not *We*.

Shelby took a step toward her. Solana shook off a handful of emotions and turned to run.

"Wait!" Shelby cried. "We need to talk!"

The ball had rolled back into Solana's path. She

tripped over it and landed flat on her side, smacking the full length of her leg against the concrete. She wailed in pain and scrambled to her feet, tried to limp away. But Shelby caught her easily with her free arm. Solana's head grew fuzzy. Her sight wavered. She fell to the ground, unconscious, without the comforting presence of Taiyo to numb her pain. She heard Shelby's voice as she drifted off, and Seth started crying.

"What on earth?" she cried when Solana collapsed at her feet. Taking full stock of the girl's tattered clothing and blood-caked leg, Shelby had a sinking feeling in her stomach. "Gerry! Get out here! I need your help!"

*　　　*　　　*

Solana woke up in the free clinic downtown. She knew it was the clinic because the smells hurt her nose—the chemical smells and the too-much-perfume smells and—somehow among all that—the smell of sickness and too little funding. That last bit, she knew all too well from the Home. Her heart raced when she thought of the Home. She gasped and sat up on the dingy cot. And almost slammed into Shelby's face.

"Solana, I'm so glad you're awake!" Shelby said, embracing Solana awkwardly.

"What happened?" Solana asked, darting her eyes everywhere in paranoia.

"Well, for starters, you fainted in front of my house," Shelby said.

Solana turned from Shelby. "Didn't know it was your house."

Shelby was quiet for a long moment. "The nurse says those wounds on your leg look like animal claw marks. Wanna tell me how you got them?"

Solana shook her head, knowing that anything she said would lead Shelby back to her place in the woods. Her heart didn't settle with Shelby's comforting voice. Her belly churned with nerves yet again. When Solana looked down at her leg, she saw layers of white gauze. The pain was gone for the moment.

"Can I go now?" she asked.

"Solana, you've been missing for weeks," Shelby said. Her cell phone rang and she answered it, speaking quietly for a few seconds. "Tommy's assistant will be on her way in a bit. You will get to go back with her."

Solana frowned. "Back to the Home, you mean?"

Shelby bowed her head. "Yes."

"No. I'm not going back," Solana said, her eyes downcast, her spirit tired of this conversation.

"But it's what's best for you," Shelby said. She took Solana's hands in hers.

Solana stared dumbly at her first kind human contact in recent memory and pulled her hands away. "Do you really believe that?"

Shelby's eyes spoke volumes. She didn't believe it anymore. When she opened her mouth to respond, her cell rang again. She listened intently. "That's a shame. I'm sorry to hear it. Are you sure? Will that be okay?"

Solana searched Shelby's face for some explanation for the happiness in her voice.

"The social worker has an emergency extraction she has to handle. And Tommy was delayed by an inspection up north. He's been pulling double duty with inspection and social work," Shelby said, her tone confidential. "Neither will be able to make it tonight!"

"So you want to take me back instead?" Solana asked, her heart sinking.

"Nope. Not my department anymore. I handle adoptions now," Shelby said. Her eyes glinted. "Tommy gave me permission to lodge you for the night, until he or his assistant can make it tomorrow. What do you say?"

Shocked, Solana said nothing. The alternative for one night's stay at Shelby's house? If she declined, Shelby would take her directly to the Home. But

Something in Shelby's face told her otherwise. Solana's eyes filled with tears. *Just one night at Shelby's house,* Solana thought. *But it'll have to be enough! But maybe, just maybe...* Solana let the hope surface once more. *Otherwise, Tommy'll have to drag me kicking and screaming back to Battelio.* Solana pulled in her pouting lip and nodded vigorously.

Then her stomach roared in hunger.

Shelby's smile fell. "When's the last time you had a full meal, kiddo?"

Solana dropped her head again. The churning in her belly betrayed her.

"Well, I have good news!" Shelby leaned in to whisper. "Gerry is an excellent cook, and he has a full roast cooking right now, with all the fixings. We'll eat like kings for days!"

Solana pressed her lips together. What if Gerry didn't like her? She picked at the hangnails on her fingers. *I'll eat like I'm part of the family for one day*, she thought. But that thought raised her spirits, if only a little.

"Doc said your scratches will be tender for a few days, that they were pretty deep in spots. But they cleaned up very well, with no infection in sight. We'll need to change the bandage every day, but other than taking out a few stitches and avoiding exerting yourself, you'll heal up just fine," Shelby said.

Solana didn't miss the word *we* in her explanation. Her heart soared, fit to burst. And though she remained apprehensive, she let her mind wander. Shelby took Solana's hand and helped her into the car, handing her the backpack with a duffle bag stuffed inside. If she wondered where Solana lost her books, Shelby didn't ask.

"Hey, there!" Gerry said when they came through the door. He bounced baby Seth on his hip, smiling brilliantly. "You're Solana, right? I've heard quite a bit about you!"

Solana dropped her head.

"She's had a long day—a long couple weeks, I'd wager," Shelby said, casting a warning look at Gerry. "And she'll be spending the night here."

The man smiled in response. "Then I bet she'd love a bite of my world-famous roast!"

"We'd both love some," Shelby said. She kissed Seth on the cheek, then Gerry. "More like, it's house-famous," she whispered to Solana. "But it is very good! Let's get you cleaned up for dinner."

Solana started shaking at the thought of getting cleaned up. Scalding water splashed over her head, stinging her skin and making her feel sick. She felt the pain of Battelio's official welcome into the Home. Her breathing raced as fast as her heart. Trembling, she couldn't take a single step forward.

"What's wrong?" Shelby said. She knelt before Solana. "We'll just wash our hands and faces for now, then, okay? We'll worry about a bath later. I'll help you if you're worried about your leg."

Solana slowed her breathing and regained control of her pulse. She nodded and let Shelby lead her into the bathroom. Shelby ran lukewarm water and dumped plenty of good-smelling soap in Solana's dirty hands. She wetted a washcloth and gently rubbed at Solana's dirty face.

"There," Shelby said, handing a towel to Solana. "Much better, right?"

Solana nodded again, feeling an odd calm settle over her. She felt out of place at the small table set for three plus one highchair for Seth. But she sat in the chair in silence while Gerry piled a generous serving of roast and vegetables on her plate. Then he led grace and encouraged her to dig in. Gerry wasn't like she imagined at all. She stared at her plate so long that Gerry came over and knelt at her side.

"Hey, Solana?" he began. "I was wondering if you know any kind of board games. Something we could play after dinner?"

Solana nodded. "I know chess."

"I have a board, if you want to play later," he said. "But you gotta eat to get up the strength to keep up with me at the game!"

Solana smiled in spite of herself, and nodded. She leaned into her meal, meek in her request for seconds. She felt quite sure she had never eaten anything so delicious. When her stomach cramped and ached from too much good food on a shrunken stomach, she apologized for gorging herself. But they laughed and chatted and dodged Seth's flying spoons and food—and included her in their conversation. Solana felt the warmth of family for the first time in years.

"Come on, sweetie," Shelby said, dangling from her shoulder Seth, who collapsed in sleep shortly after dinner. "Gerry will load the dishwasher, then get out the chessboard. Meanwhile, let's get you into the bath."

Despite her trust in Shelby on the matter, Solana's heart pounded. She hated bathtubs more than almost anything. But perhaps it would be different tonight. *She didn't hurt me earlier*, Solana remembered. But the trembling began again. She stared at the tub in the bathroom, unable to move.

Shelby laid Seth in his crib in the nursery. Then she returned to Solana, who still stared at the empty bathtub. Brushing past the little girl, she turned on the water, testing the temperature on her wrist. "Is this warm enough, Solana?"

Solana snapped out of her reverie and reached her hand out. The water was warm, but not too hot. "Yes," she answered. "It won't burn at all."

Shelby turned and looked into Solana's eyes. "Did you get burnt by the bath before?"

Solana nodded. "Don't wanna talk about it, though."

Shelby worked her jaw in anger at the prospect of scalding bathwater. She took a deep breath. "Let's get you out of these clothes, okay?"

Solana set her backpack in the corner and handed Shelby all her clothes. She pulled a tattered, folded piece of paper from one pocket, and a compass from the other. These she set with her backpack. She took down her dirty pigtails. Then she stepped into the warm water. Her heart settled down, finally.

Shelby helped her prop her injured leg on the edge of the tub, made sure she had shampoo and soap and towels, then left her to her bathing.

"Call me if you need anything at all!" she said.

Solana sat in the warm water for a long time, motionless, trying to deduce reality from fantasy. At long last, she began soaping her arms, her uninjured leg, torso and hair. She paid particular attention to the back of her neck and ears, since those hadn't been properly cleaned with soap since she left. As she bathed, the enormity of her last two weeks, and last years, overwhelmed her. She cried and cried, muffling the sounds against her arm lest Shelby should hear her. Something had broken inside, and she couldn't mend it.

*   *   *

"No, Tommy, I'm telling you," Shelby whispered harshly, "something went on at that house with this girl. And it's foolish to think that the other children fared any better."

She listened silently, working her jaw in anger. "If you can't do something about it, I will!" She pressed END, wishing fervently that she could slam a real receiver on a hook, as in the old days of hanging up a phone. She tapped the phone against her forehead. Leaning against the wall, she heard Solana pull the drain on her bathwater. Putting on her best smile, she knocked on the door.

"Need help, kiddo?"

"Maybe, in a minute," Solana said.

Shelby heard splashing and squeaking against the sides of the tub. "Now?" she asked.

"Maybe," Solana answered. "Okay, yes!"

Shelby opened the door and scooped Solana out of the tub. She set her down on her feet and wrapped a towel around her. "There," she said. "Do you feel better now?"

Solana's haunted eyes grew distant for a moment, remembering the flickering images of bathtime at her own home, years ago. "Yes, I think so." Solana snatched her backpack from the corner, and scrambled to pick up the folded piece of paper and her compass.

"I'm glad," she said, leading her down the hall to a spacious bedroom with ornate wallpaper and a large four-post bed. "Now let's get you dressed for game time. Gerry's waiting!"

"Is it okay if I sit on your couch in those pants? They were dirty." Solana sounded ashamed and nervous.

"Well, I wouldn't mind," Shelby answered. "But I was hoping you'd like what I picked out for you here." The woman knelt in front of her closet. Out of a heavy-duty garbage bag, she pulled shirts and pants, socks and shoes, jackets and scarves. "I picked these up from the donation center a couple days back, for little girls who need them. I already put them through the washer and dryer. I'm just glad I didn't pass them on yet!"

"I can have a whole outfit?" Solana asked, starry-eyed. She knelt by the bag.

"You can have as much as you want, sweetie," Shelby said, her voice so soft and sweet that Solana trembled in emotion.

Solana looked down at the clean clothes until they blurred in her sight. Big tears dropped on her hands. She hugged the little jeans to her face long enough to drench the leg, willing her body to stop betraying her heart.

"It'll be okay, Solana," Shelby said. "I promise."

Solana nodded, still cramming the pant leg against her face. Shelby wrapped her arms around the little girl, holding her tight until her tears subsided into an occasional hiccup. So much fell into place about Solana's reasoning, actions and reactions. She couldn't control the very real physical reaction she had to the bathtub. Shelby intended to get to the bottom of the matter, before time ran out for Solana.

*   *   *

Gerry stared intently at the board before him. He leaned forward from the couch, pursing his lips, folding his hands, glaring at the pieces, leaning back against the cushions and then repeating the actions again. On occasion, he'd move a chess piece. Without hesitation, Solana would move hers immediately afterward. It proved a silent game for them both.

Solana beat Gerry soundly at chess every single time, without effort. She noticed at first, thinking he would simply indulge his guest, he made silly mistakes. But an hour into match after match leading to his defeat, he dove into strategy with gusto. Finally, consenting to her supremacy at the King's game, he threw up his hands with a laugh.

"Checkmate! Again...You got me, kid!" Gerry said. He flipped his king on its side with a chuckle. He leaned in with a confidential tone, "So what's your secret?"

Solana thought about his question for a long time. "I don't have a secret. Pieces can only move certain ways with the same goal. But I try to make them tell the best story they can with what they have, every time!" She smiled at him. The grin didn't quite reach her eyes, but it was close.

"So I lost to the story?" Gerry said.

"No," Solana said, her face a mask of seriousness. "You were a part of it!"

Speechless, he stared at her. Then he smiled. "You're a very smart girl, aren't you?"

Solana ducked her head in embarrassment.

"Bedtime, you two." Shelby swept in, wearing pajamas and a robe. "This is for you, Solana." She handed the girl a bundled blanket and a pillow. "This couch is the softest bed in the house!" She shooed Gerry away from the couch and tucked a soft cotton sheet into the cushions.

"Thank you," Solana said, implying more than just the bed.

"I want you to have the best night's sleep," Shelby said. "We have a busy day tomorrow!"

"Oh," Solana said. She squeezed the pillow, stroked the blanket, and avoided Shelby's eyes.

"Tommy and I are going to have a long talk, Solana," she answered. "So rest assured that I'll do everything I can to help."

Solana nodded and climbed into her makeshift bed, pushing down the thousand questions that arose, and pushing down hope. Shelby spread the cover over her, tucked the pillow behind her head, and kissed her forehead. "Rest," she ordered.

"Thank you, Gerry," Solana rolled to her side and craned her neck to see him. "That was the best story time in years!"

"You're welcome, little lady," Gerry answered softly. "But you taught me a thing or two!"

She liked this little dream of hers, so much that it broke her heart to hope for it. She smiled at him once more, sighed and relaxed. She closed her eyes, smiling, and imagined, in this dream, falling asleep almost instantly, safe in the arms of this sweet, loving home. But the comfortable couch-bed kept her awake. It wasn't firm like her pine boughs. It wasn't her bed.

And this was all just a dream she entertained, just for the day. When they turned off the overhead lights and left the room, she opened her eyes on a ceiling fan, on the white pebble texture of the ceiling, and listened to the intense, quiet conversation coming from their bedroom for a long time. She couldn't hear the words, just the tone. She waited a long time for them to finally turn off their lamps and sleep.

*   *   *

Shelby wandered into the kitchen early the next morning and started the coffee pot. Seth still snored lightly in the next room, so she had a few minutes to herself. She yawned and raked back her dark hair, trying to wake up. Then she realized something was amiss.

She remembered the long talk she had with Gerry about Solana, after she fell asleep. Her heart pounded. Across the counter, she saw into the living room. But Solana wasn't sleeping on the couch. In fact, the couch had been tidied up. The blanket, pillow and sheet were missing, as was Solana's backpack. Her heart fluttered with a hundred worries.

Shelby ran back to the bedroom. "Gerry! Wake up! She's gone," she said.

"She who?" Gerry mumbled. "Oh, Solana?"

"Get up, but be quiet! Don't wake Seth just yet," Shelby hissed.

When Gerry joined her, Shelby had stopped at the refrigerator door. A handwritten note hung on the door by a magnet, with the letters IOU scrawled at the top, with Solana signing as the indebted recipient of goods. Beneath that, Shelby read a list of goods: "Two outfits (thank you so much!), an extra pair of shoes, the pajamas I wore, a blanket, a sheet, and a pillow (because these were torn up by Bob)—who's Bob?— some bandages and antibiotic ointment, some canned food and a couple water bottles, one saucepan, and just a little bit of Gerry's yummy roast."

"Is this kid for real? Where would she have gone?"

Gerry asked. "That leg was hurt pretty badly."

Shelby shook her head. Tears sprung to her eyes. "She promises to replace or pay for everything she took, just as soon as she can, so please don't consider it stealing. Because she doesn't like stealing at all, and doesn't think her mommy and dad would approve of it."

Gerry hugged Shelby close to his side, and read over her shoulder, "I'm sorry I caused you any problems. Please tell them it's all my fault so you don't get in trouble. Thank you so much for reminding me what family feels like! I just can't go back to the Home, no matter what. Please don't hate me for that, because I still love you and know you don't want me to be hurt. Merry Christmas and Happy New Year! Love, Solana. P.S. Maybe, when I'm older, can I come see you again, if I'm welcome? I promise to tell the best stories by then!"

Shelby felt Gerry's tears on her shoulder. He wept openly into her neck. "I have been an idiot this whole time. I should have supported you when you first asked me about her. I was just too prideful, too selfish to listen. She's such a wonderful little girl. And now she's out there alone somewhere. It's all my fault!"

"No. It's my fault." Shelby wiped her eyes with the back of her arm. "She doesn't know that we were going to fight to keep her this time." Shelby scoffed, feeling every moment a fool. "I doubt she would've believed it if I told her."

"Do you think we could catch up to her?" Gerry asked. "How long ago do you think she woke up?"

Shelby laughed bitterly. The realization dawned on her. "She's smart, Gerry. You honestly think she went to sleep that quickly?"

"She just waited until we fell asleep," Gerry said, suppressing a ball of anger and hurt and guilt into determination. "She's been gone six or seven hours? There has to be a way to track her." Gerry stormed over to the couch, looking this way and that for some sign that would help them find her. "I mean, she wants to have a family, right? She can't want to be alone!"

From the nursery, Seth cried, having awoken to yelling from the next room.

"It doesn't matter what she wants, in her mind," Shelby said, her voice hollow. "It only matters that others didn't want her. That we didn't want her. That we rejected her then. She thought we were just going to haul her off tomorrow, and go on enjoying our perfect little lives without her!" Shelby broke down, crying and screaming. "It's all my fault!" She flung chairs right and left, laid hold of couch cushions and flung them across the room.

Helpless, Gerry stood watching, clenching and unclenching his fists. Nothing he said calmed her. She shrugged off his embrace and said things he knew she didn't mean. He waited out this unprecedented storm, making sure Shelby wouldn't hurt herself. When his wife began to run out of steam, Gerry breathed again. When Seth cried out again, Gerry went to him, leaving Shelby to shoulder her guilt.

Finally exhausted, she sank into the floor by the couch, sobbing into her bare hands. Wordless noise flooded her mouth until finally she curled against the couch, wheezing on occasion as one does after crying hard. She lost track of how long she shivered there.

She let her hands fall in front of her face. She flexed her fingers under the couch. They tingled from exertion. But her fingertips brushed against a thin square object wedged between the couch and the floor. She pulled out a tattered piece of folded paper as big as her palm. Recognizing it as the carefully guarded paper Solana carried, she unfolded it. She gasped.

"Gerry! Get in here!" Shelby cried.

Her husband ran in, Seth—freshly diapered and chattering—on his hip. He leaned over a piece of rough-looking art paper. Trees and streams, buildings and landmarks had been laid out in a pattern all over the surface. Between each item curved rows of dots, hearts, diamonds and other shapes in red and arrows that pointed in confusing angles. Toward the top of the page, in a clearing indicated by a scribble of light green, set a bright red star with a little tent drawn beside it.

"That's her home, isn't it, up in the woods?" Gerry asked. Seth reached for the paper, but Gerry pulled him back. "And there's Bob with a cat's face. Does that mean a bobcat caused the wounds on her leg? He's not that far from her home either. She could be in danger. Doesn't look like there's a legend, though, so we don't know what increment she used."

"We'll figure it out," Shelby said. "We have to, so we can get her back."

Shelby's cell rang. Gerry looked at the caller identification and sighed.

"So Shel? What are you going to tell Tommy?"

"That she ran away again. That she's a scared, troubled young girl whose negligent and abusive treatment by employees at Sunny Creek resulted in her disappearance. That I will petition for a thorough, unbiased evaluation of the facilities and staff," Shelby answered bitterly. "And that if Solana ever comes into custody of the state again, I—we—will claim full parental rights in the absence of her biological parents."

"Better say most of that in person, so he can fire you to you face!" Gerry chuckled.

"Then I'll start with reporting her missing," Shelby said, reaching for her phone.

"That's a good start. She's had plenty of time to disappear." Gerry asked, "And about the map?"

"What map?" Shelby said with a smile, waving the piece of paper in the air. "Solana will be our daughter. We have to convince her of that fact. But we have to find her first."

"Any chance she left this on purpose, so we could come looking for her?" Gerry asked.

"No. Not Solana," Shelby said. "We burnt this

bridge, and all she knows how to do is move forward and survive. Her whole life is a story. She barrels ahead, but she lets it guide her."

"If that's the case, I know how to decode this map," said Gerry. He handed over Seth to Shelby and took the map. Laying it on the kitchen island alongside Solana's goodbye note, he grabbed a pen and notepad. He drew out each of the symbols in a list down the side of the page.

"I'd bet, to keep herself company, Solana tells stories to pass the time," Gerry said.

Shelby agreed. "But that doesn't explain her map."

"Yes, it does," Gerry said. "What if each symbol is a different story?"

"Oh, my!" Shelby cried. "Then she would start the story when she left her base and finish it by the time she got back. You're a genius!"

"Not quite. She's still got us beat," Gerry admitted. "Until we know which symbol goes to which story, and then know the story and how long it would take to tell it. That's not counting the natural evolution of the story as she repeated it!"

"True, but there are some stories she would know better than others," Shelby said, and explained Solana's omnipresent books. "She didn't have them with her today, which means she left them somewhere. And if she had sense enough to leave them, anticipating a load of supplies, then she probably left them at the Home for the same reason. If we find the books, we can break her code."

"What do you say, Seth?" Gerry asked. "Let's go find your sister!"

10: RECRUITING FATE

Solana tried to stay devoted to her new life as a mountain girl. She wondered on occasion if leaving Shelby and Gerry was the right thing to do. But they told her more than once she would go back to the Home when Tommy came by. She couldn't risk it. She wouldn't give in to her flights of fancy again. They had already made their choice. Anything else was a self-told lie. She only regretted her lost map. She had since busied herself drawing another, but it wasn't the same. But if that map proved to be her only regret in all this, then she could rest easy.

Since her flight from the Home, two more months passed in much the same boring manner. Thanksgiving was over the day she left. Shortly after she fled Shelby and Gerry, Christmas came and went, along with New Year's Day since. The anticipation of the snowfall was the coldest she'd ever been. She feared losing consciousness several times. When snow finally came, the bitterness of the dry cold lifted a bit. The first light snows fell, followed by the second and third heavier snows.

Solana only left her small home into the wet cold

when the snow fell lightly, or not at all, or when she needed to relieve herself. She kept a blazing fire as often as she could in the big hearth, and needed to gather wood and water daily. She used a rock to bust the thick ice covering the spring and filled her bottles with the icy water. Then she returned to her little settlement and dried her shoes in front of the fire. She ate a little, then daydreamed and warmed herself and missed the company of her books. She even used a little sweetened condensed milk to make snowcream a few times. She piled blessings upon Shelby and Gerry forever for small comforts like that, though she'd borrowed the canned goods, clothing and bed stuff without permission.

Today, it snowed—heavier than she ever remembered. The temperature dipped so low that she could only curl up in a ball in her blanket and shiver. She tried to cover the hot ashes in the big fire with stones so she only had to stoke it when the snow stopped, but she also had to move a smaller fire into her doorway. She left a crack for the smoke to get out and piled twigs on it to keep it going. She held her hands close to warm them, often passing her hands through the flames and then pressing the warmth against her face. Her fiery hair slid forward around her neck and glowed in the misty dim light from outside and the small flickering light inside.

Her aches and pains and hunger her constant companions, she moved as little as possible to conserve energy. Feeling the beginnings of despair, regret, worry and doubt creep in, she forced her body up and out of the lean-to. She brought in her water to keep it from freezing and bursting. She took a few drinks and pulled the blanket tighter around her. She eyed her bottle of diluted soup. Her stomach growled in malnourished pain, and she justified needing a little more food in colder weather. Starving in that moment, she drank the tomato soup straight down.

Mid-gulp, Solana froze at an unnatural sound

outside her door. Above the low howling of the wind rose another, more regular sound. She felt afraid, having encountered few animals in her journey, and none that could hurt her except Bob. She thought perhaps it could be some hungry animal growling and prowling. Then she heard a definitive trudging through the snow. Something walked her way. She chanced a glance out the crack in her door.

She only saw the snow piled in drifts across the small area that she cleared for her fire. She imagined it had to be piled heavily across her rickety house as well, a house that could not protect her against a big animal that wanted an easy meal. Solana quietly wedged herself into the back corner of her lean-to, scooting on a few walnuts left in her depleted stash and forsaking her fire in search of some measure of safety. She watched the flame flicker in the breeze and fight to stay alive. A heavy gust pulled at the thin timbers and snuffed out the fire. Heavy gray smoke billowed out the crack in the door.

Then she heard someone speaking, and a fear greater than fear of dangerous animals rose in Solana's chest. Her heart beat fiercely. High narrow walls closed in around her. Blackness darker than night blotted out her vision. She became lost in the memory of The Cell where she spent so many days. Her all-too-vivid imagination decided her painful punishment before Solana even knew who was outside her small shelter. A female voice floated through the bitter air—a voice both gentle and determined. Then a man spoke, his baritone voice low and resonant. Solana did not recognize the voices, which almost scared her more. Then she realized the odd quality of the syllables and tones, the combinations of musical words and flowing cadence. The language was not the same as hers. Almost familiar, but nowhere near the same. *In fact,* she mused in her detached way, *the words sound like no single human tongue I've heard.*

Solana roused from her fascination by heavy footsteps outside her small door. The smoke from the extinguished fire had begun to dissipate, but wafted back into her small enclosure to sting her eyes and throat. She pressed her lips together to suppress the cough that threatened and blinked away the heavy tears that flowed from her eyes. A low voice, the woman's sweet words, reached her ears now. The words seemed to be entreating her, coaxing her out. Solana realized she was being called. The tomato juice bottle spilled some of its contents onto her hand. She had clenched it tightly enough to dent the sides. It was almost her last bottle of food.

"No! Go away! I don't want to go back!" Solana shouted in her most valiant voice. She bit her lips together in shock at the hate in her words.

The voice came again, more sincere and deliberate.

"No!" screamed the frightened girl. "I'm not going back to there! I would die and be with my Mommy and Dad first!" Her nervous high pitch made her sound even younger than she was. But the fury still shook her.

A moment passed in silence. *Maybe they will really leave*, Solana had begun to think. Then an expression much like the human "Well, all right then" sounded from the female voice. The words were full of pain and softly spoken. A few breaths later Solana heard a few low words mumbled by several voices. The male voice cut through with its odd self-conscious quality.

A few seconds later, Solana heard three very quick thuds on the ground. Before she realized they were footsteps, she heard what sounded like metal slicing into wood in two clean strokes. Her jaw fell open beneath wide eyes as the roof of her small lean-to fell apart in the middle and the whole thing—base trees and all—was whisked away in the wake of a powerful wind. The soft thud of the wood as it landed a few feet away registered somewhere in her mind, but her eyes immediately found the man who had caused the destruction of her small house.

He stood facing her, his long black hair pulled straight out to his right in the gust of his own making. Also on his right he held in both hands a huge heavy-looking sword, longer than he was tall and horizontal to the ground, still held aloft from his final stroke. He wore a black tank shirt and dark pants. The wind pulled at the thick gray cloak draped across his shoulders. Heavy black boots and a belt, as well as a strap of leather across his chest, completed his attire.

In a series of fluid movements, he settled out of the menacing battle stance, pulled his shoulders back and, with one hand, replaced the huge sword into a holster on his back. His black hair finally settled around his face and shoulders. Through the strands, the entranced Solana saw his black mournful eyes set at an upward slant and his grim mouth with lips pressed together. For a long time he was all she could see. Without taking her eyes off his, she could make out the bare shoulders and scarred, muscular arms under the shielding fabric of his cape. He looked human enough to her. When, for just a second, his eyes actually gazed back at her, she saw something disturbing there. He looked at her with a profound sorrow that, even in her early youth, wrenched her heart into reality. He looked away with great effort, to his left. He stared silently at someone there.

Solana shook her head and coughed a little. All that transpired in the minute since her house was hacked to pieces by the man dissipated when she regained her fiery composure. She stalked over and stood defiantly in front of the sad young man.

"I won't go. I won't go back," she said with all the menace her high-pitched voice could muster, punctuating each word with a finger poke to the man's belly, for that's as high as she could reach.

A quiet rippling laugh echoed through the new silence. The sound was reassuring and apologetic. Solana's eyes moved of their own accord to the source. A tall woman stood in the falling snow, looking more like a statue than a real person. Her skin shimmered as radiantly as the snow that surrounded her. For all the bitter cold she had not dressed in warm clothes, wearing only a translucent, loosely fitting violet robe. In stark contrast flowed her long, sleek ebony hair. Her amethyst eyes entranced Solana. The woman's pink mouth spared a sad smile.

"So young, yet her heart flames within her," the statue-lady said in the foreign tongue. "I do believe it's her, for who else could it be?"

Solana did not understand the foreign words. She picked up instead on the buried weariness and staggering hope the delicate voice projected. Then the voice spoke to her, but the lady's lips did not move. Solana could understand. A torrent of images spun through her mind. The visuals flowed in a linear pattern that Solana soon was able to interpret.

She saw another place, another world. She saw a long journey made in desperation, the gathering of forces against unknown enemies—she saw war and devastation. There was a flicker of familiarity in those memories, a face in recent memory that looked a lot like Archer's. Solana turned her thoughts toward him. He dressed differently, but she knew those eyes, his face, his white hair, even his eyeglasses. And he wasn't in distress or pain that she caused, it seemed. She helped him, brought him into a healing room and protected him. Solana's heart soared with a different kind of hope. Apparently, she had seen too much of this mind-voice she sensed from the sparkling woman, for the lady tore her eyes away. The wordless barrage stopped.

"You know that man?" Solana pressed. "You know Archer?"

Solana stared at her, puzzling over what she'd

seen. She tucked her chin in defiance and regarded the statue lady with intelligent curiosity. The woman nodded. Solana bounced on her feet, exhaustion forgotten in the excitement.

"Are you Taiyo?" Solana asked with bright-eyed giddiness.

"Taiyo?" the woman responded. She made a slight movement with her head that meant "no" in the girl's language, then reached out her hand to the child as she shivered in the frozen whiteness.

Solana found something she could trust in the woman's sad smile, and in her knowledge and treatment of Archer, if the mind stuff could be trusted and not a trick. She didn't know how long ago the woman had known him, or if he somehow lived still. She hoped fervently.

The young man seemed troubled as well, but not hostile toward her. She then noticed several men around her with strange dark complexions and wild flaxen hair. Their eyes looked unnaturally luminescent with only a hint of color, with a cleft of flesh above their eyelids that made them look racially related. One of these men appeared very young, with almost catlike features and a long scar across his nose. He looked at her in blatant curiosity, his expressive eyes understanding a great deal about Solana at a glance. She stared back. Her gut expressed nothing but safety.

She glanced back at the woman. "I don't think you're an angel, either," Solana reasoned.

"Briescha," was the answer she received.

Solana hesitated. "From that pretty place I saw in my head?"

"Azela," Briescha answered.

Solana turned and looked at her ruined lean-to. "I don't have anywhere to stay now. Can I come with you? Maybe get help finding Taiyo?"

Briescha nodded, with a ghost of a smile on her pink lips.

Shivering, Solana crept back into her lean-to, tossing rubble carelessly out of the way. She felt the young scarred man's eyes on her back as she pushed aside the splintered wood. She didn't want him to feel bad about what he'd done, but there was something she couldn't leave behind. The young man with the cat-like face appeared at her side and started moving aside pieces of splintered wood. Finally, her hand settled on a canvas strap. Solana hauled out her backpack and pulled her locket from the front pocket. She tied it around her throat. Solana slung her empty bag across her back and trudged across the snow to the lady, to Briescha with her outstretched hand. The boy rejoined the others with a smile.

With a final glance back, Solana felt herself going down yet another new path, one stranger than any other, but one that put her more at peace than any other. She put her hand in Briescha's and felt a deep sense of security as the men, led by the dark-haired youth, fell into step around them. Still, his eyes followed her: not angry, but sorrowful. Full of loss. Solana seemed to be a reminder of something he may rather forget. She turned to him with a smile, seeing his surprise at being caught, and smiling bigger, her dimples setting off her radiant grin as much as her glowing eyes. He hurt. She felt it choking him.

Her hand snapped out without a thought and closed around his first and middle fingers. He initially tried to pull away, but she would not let go. She swung his arm to and fro by his fingers and held fast with her cold little hand, in her innocence deciding to pull him from his sorrow the only way she knew how—with childish sweetness. He eventually gave in to her playful swinging of his arm, but wouldn't dare pretend to enjoy it. Solana had promised Mommy and Dad through God that she would share the love she had been given. Maybe this was one of the chances He'd given her to make good on that promise. Even when her arm felt cold and numb, she wouldn't let go. She had a promise to keep.

Her steps began to drag from weariness and lack of food a long way from her little camp. Her eyes blurry from exhaustion, she would not complain. When she began to stumble and shiver in the cold, she felt strong hands pull her to her feet, then lift her into the air. Solana came to rest on a hard, living surface: her head lying on someone's shoulder. Instinctively, she turned her round face toward the warmth of the man's neck. He smelled somehow familiar, maybe like Archer. She instantly relaxed where he held her. Her little arms reached around his neck and clasped behind him. Straight black hair fell in front of her sleepy eyes and warmed her face. She felt muscular arms that she knew were nicked with pink and white scars hold her protectively as she drifted off to exhausted sleep. *The young man is carrying me.* Then a dreaming smile drifted onto her lips as she slept soundly in the cradle of his arms.

Solana opened her heavy eyes on the falling darkness. Her stomach growled. All the glamour and mystique of her adventure had drained away in her great fatigue and malnourishment. The hunger began gnawing again. When she heard her stomach again, she tensed, afraid that she may become a burden to those who had taken her if she wasn't strong enough to hide her hunger.

The scarred arms tightened around her. He spoke softly to someone behind him. Solana heard a rustling of cloth as someone dug something out of his carry-bag. He shifted her weight to one strong arm. His other hand waved a small block of good smelling travel food under her nose. She looked up at the youth's face. His expression was all business, with a hint of softness in his eyes. Her small cold fingers wrapped around the little slab of food and she put it to her lips. When she'd choked down the food—which had a smooth texture and sweet taste—she felt like she'd never had a better meal. She began to feel a fuzzy feeling in her stomach, like butterflies that couldn't get out. She thought it was her shrunken stomach and lack of solid food that made the fluttering. Soon, the feeling went away and she felt immensely satiated from just the small block. The special food left her feeling sleepy again. She thanked her bearer and snuggled against his neck again as they trekked on.

A familiar voice awakened Solana some time later. She panicked, sure that her ordeal had been a dream. But she felt the young man's strong arms holding her securely and knew she was truly safe. But the voice didn't belong out in the woods. It belonged to a woman wearing a crisp white shirt.

"Shelby?" Solana said, groggy. "What are you doing out here?"

Shelby Ellington stood in the snow with her long dark hair disheveled, blowing in the stiff breeze. She clung to a long heavy coat and carried a large flashlight. She looked panicky. Gerry stumbled out of the woods behind her, cursing the brambles.

"What in the world?" Gerry cried. "Who are these people?"

"Looking for you, Solana!" Shelby said, rushing forward. "I can't believe that it's you! We figured out your map code! This is your stand of nut trees. We've been looking for you all this time! It was so cold, we were worried you would be in danger. But here you are, alive and well!"

"You found me. Thank you," Solana said with a sleepy grin. Then she yawned. "But you're too late."

"No, Solana! I'm here. We're here," Shelby said, turning to Gerry and waving a piece of paper over her head. Solana recognized her tattered map. "I made a huge mistake. Can you forgive me? Can you come home with us right now and forget all about it? Will you be part of our family, our daughter?"

"I forgive you, always! Shelby, I love you, and Gerry, and little Seth." Solana perked up, awake and realizing that Shelby really had found her. "But you're too late for the rest of it. And that's okay, too."

Shelby stepped forward with her arms out, looking at the group all around Solana. The young man took a step back defensively.

"I love you, too. But what do you mean?" Shelby asked Solana.

"I've got to go now." Tears welled in Solana's eyes, then spilled down her cheeks. For a long moment, she longed for Shelby's home with Gerry and Seth. Her heart felt so full all of a sudden. She didn't want Shelby to hurt. But this was an adventure, and what a story she would tell! "Go and be the best mommy ever! I promise I'll come back to visit when I can. I owe you, after all. And I'll have the best stories ever to tell you!"

"Wait! Don't go, Solana, please!" Shelby cried out. "I'll fix that awful place! I'll fix the whole thing from the top down, so that no one will ever hurt anyone there again! Just please, don't go."

Dreaming or not, Solana believed her. Shelby would keep her word. She found comfort in that, and finally let herself drift back toward sleep.

"And please, don't hurt her." Shelby reached for Solana. The young man easily maneuvered out of her grasp. "Tell me what you want with her! Where are you taking her?"

The young man looked toward Brieschia, who watched the Shelby woman intently. Then her pink lips parted in a smile. She stared up at the sky and pointed to the stars.

The Shelby woman stared incoherently for a long moment. Then, wide-eyed, she crumpled to the ground, burying her face in her hands. Solana still dripped tears in a steady stream down the young man's chest.

What a nice dream! If freezing to death is this much of a story, then she'd have a great one to tell her parents when she saw them again. Sleepy Solana decided it was nice to have Shelby come for her in the end. But something new had claimed her without reservations. And this something already saved her life, fed her, and showed kindness to her without even knowing her situation.

Solana sighed, snuggled closer to the young man's throat, and collapsed in a contented sleep, ready for the next stage in her adventure.

Ready for more? The story continues in
Ariana, Book 4, A Novella of the Pathos Series,
Available in Kindle Unlimited, Audible, and Paperback!

ABOUT THE AUTHOR

Tamara Henson lives in Kentucky with her precious little family, and all the people in her head. She's devoted to her son Elric and her man Will, and her kitty-brat Twitter-pater. She's a Sci-fi/Fantasy Author and Artist, Anime/Manga Fan, Legal Stabber of Tattoo and Piercing Clients, a Directionally-Challenged and Incompetent Gamer Gal, and a Workaholic Entrepreneur. Always improving, except in gaming, probably.

She is likely working on something creative, when she should be sleeping.

To access exclusive info and offers related to Tamara's PATHOS universe, go to her website:

www.tamarahenson.com

Discover other Pathos Series titles by Tamara Henson:

- Rowan Jun (Book 1)
- Silver Empress (Pathos, Book 2)
- Ariana (Pathos, Book 4, A Novella)
- Primorda (Book 5) *Fall, 2026*
- Incarnata (Book 6) *Spring, 2027*

Discover 3 NEW Romance Series by Tamara Henson (Series Titles TBA):

Cryptid (w/ a JACKALOPE SHIFTER!!), *Fall, 2026*
Dystopian and Dark Fae Romance Series
TITLES TO BE ANNOUNCED, COMING SOON!

<u>ABOUT THE PATHOS SERIES:</u>

Tamara Henson's ever-expanding Pathos universe spans space and dimensions beyond the waking world to bring fresh life to mythologies, folklore, and legends, spinning epic original locations and memorable, multi-dimensional characters in rich detail with her playful dialogue and direct writing style.

Join Rowan Jun in his path toward redemption from slave to warrior.

Walk the path of Briescha, a born diplomat so dedicated to her sister that she would shatter the cosmos to keep her safe.

Follow Solana into the wilderness as she escapes those who seek to harm her, and follows the voice of the mysterious Taiyo of the Flames.

Let Ariana guide you through her new life in the Mansion in the Mountain, where the mystery of her family is finally revealed, and her true trial begins.

Tread the path toward life and redemption, where suffering and pain hold the promise of a brighter, more joyful future. The Pathos Series!

Join the tamarahenson.com newsletter for updates on all Tamara's Upcoming Projects!

SOLANA